TH

'It won't be any
hopeless. There's
know it.'

'Salmonella and friends.' Mike unscrewed a water-container, filled the kettle and put it on the stove to boil.

'Much more than that. Much more. Oh, Mike, I'm so frightened.'

He did not reply. Because he was frightened too, against all logic, all reasoning. Because he knew that the stench which had come up at him out of the well the other day had been a *living* force, an evil entity.

And whatever it was, it was still down there. Waiting. For what?

Also in Arrow by Guy N. Smith

Abomination
Accursed
Alligators
Bloodshow
Cannibals
Deathbell
Demons
Doomflight
Entombed
The Island
Manitou Doll
The Master
Satan's Snowdrop

THE FESTERING

Guy N. Smith

ARROW BOOKS

Arrow Books Limited
62–65 Chandos Place, London WC2N 4NW

An imprint of Century Hutchinson Limited

London Melbourne Sydney Auckland
Johannesburg and agencies
throughout the world.

First published in 1989

Filmset by Deltatype Limited, Ellesmere Port
Printed and bound in Great Britain by
Courier International, Tiptree, Essex

ISBN 0 09 961080 9

For Charles L. Grant.
A good friend and one of my favourite authors.

PROLOGUE

The girl had lain upon the rocky shelf on the outskirts of the tiny village daily from morning until evening, from spring through to early autumn when the leaves on the giant oaks lining the road began to show the first signs of fading. Intent, she watched the road that stretched ahead of her across the flat moorland beneath the surrounding mountains, squinting in bright sunlight, peering as dusk approached, never once leaving her position. Hope – there was always hope, interspersed with disappointment and frustration when a rider approached and came close enough so that she could see that it was not the tall rangy man for whom she waited. Tears moistened her dark eyes, trickled slowly down the dirt-smudged cheeks; dried. Perhaps the next time it would be Tabor. She knew he would come, for he had promised to return and she had never known him to break his word. Not to her, anyway.

Long dark matted hair straggled around her shoulders and became entangled with the threadbare hessian dress, a scant garment that failed to screen her shapely adolescent body from prying male eyes. The young men in the village of Garth, this forgotten hamlet of tumbledown hovels, lusted for her; she was only too well aware of that. Their grimy fingers groped her if she was not quick enough to dodge them, stroking her tender flesh where it showed through the holes in her dress. Each and every one of them prayed that some misfortune had befallen the handsome forester, whom they had cause to hate for more reasons than that he had ofttimes lain with this comely wench. On moonlit nights during the winter months stealthy poachers glanced frequently over their shoulders, uneasy in case Tabor should suddenly rear up out of the bole of some huge tree where he had been lying in wait for those who dared to steal his master's game. Tabor the Terrible, Nemesis of poachers – the legend was already growing.

The girl called Rachel saw him in her mind: his rippling muscles, not an ounce of surplus fat on his body when he disrobed himself to take her; blue eyes that shone with love in the reflected moonlight; his lips soft and warm as they crushed her own; tender and yet strong as he took her. Sometimes the memory of him was too much and she sobbed herself to sleep in her filthy sacking bed in the corner of her parents' single-roomed cottage.

'Stop tha' bawling, lass,' her father would grunt in the darkness, 'and get thee to sleep, for Tabor'll na' come back, and there'll be none in the Garth, save yersel, who'll mourn his absence. The fellow has gone to London in search of whores, they say, and I, for one, believe the talk. And shame on you for giving yourself to him when there's plenty o' decent young men in the village.'

Rachel clamped her lips together tightly, for to reply was futile. If an argument developed, her father was more than likely to take his frayed leather belt to her. Her mother would slap her, too – retribution for hurt peasant pride because their daughter had shamed them. When Tabor returned it would be different, she promised herself, for none dared to confront him openly; they whispered hatred and jealousy behind closed doors, and even then their frightened eyes darted furtively about them in case he was hidden in the shadows. A feared man, only the foolish and the brave faced him – and there were precious few of the latter in Garth.

Each morning as she walked up to the rock, she felt contemptuous eyes searing her back and knew what the villagers were saying, even if she could not hear them. 'She'll be a scrawny hag, as withered as a winter apple before Tabor returns. He'll not come back, he'll spend his strength in the brothels and be thrown out to die of the pox in the gutters. Let his soul rot in the filth of their slop buckets. . . . *if* he has a soul.'

Up on the ledge, day after day, she clung to her undying hope that Tabor would come riding back down the road, hunched over his bony nag, his clothing dusty with travel, his strong body weary. Or perhaps riding a fine horse because he had found his fortune in London and returned to claim his bride. Whatever, rich or poor, he would come back, she did not doubt. And until he did, she would watch for him.

One day she was sheltering beneath the thick rhododendron bush which offered the only protection from the keen autumnal wind. By her side was a crust of stale bread and a cold boiled potato; she ate to give her body nourishment to survive the long watch, for no other reason. Her appetite had long ago deserted her.

A rider; she stiffened, straining her tired eyes into the distant haze of a late September mist. Dust clouds and gathering fog allowed only a silhouette: a cantering mount, its rider sitting erect. Rachel groaned her frustration long before she was able to discern the aquiline features of the short, stocky man who collected the tithes from the inhabitants of Garth. Another hated one. She shrank back into the foliage, and felt the urge to cry. Hopes raised and dashed; it would happen maybe a hundred times or more before the one for whom she watched rode back into the valley. For Tabor would come. One day.

A sudden fear assailed her. The time of year was nigh for the coming of the Witchfinder. Each autumn the tall thin man wearing a wide-brimmed black hat with flowing robes to match came down the mountain road. His features were near skeletal: hollowed eyes that sought you out, burned right into your soul, located your innermost guilt so that you trembled. His questions were hissed like the pot boiling on the fire rather than spoken, demanding answers. If you lied, he knew. And if Satan lurked within a human body, then that body was destroyed. Always there was a guilty one; if not, then a scapegoat. Two years ago this man had hanged Jason, who was ageing and was surely near his time, anyway. The old man had sworn his innocence, but when the heated iron singed his flesh he confessed – and screamed for mercy as his fellow villagers dragged him to the hanging tree on the outskirts of Garth and tightened the noose around his sinewy neck, throwing the loose end of the rope over the thick bough. Three men had hauled the struggling, kicking body aloft until the blistered feet were well clear of the ground, then wound the hemp around a stump to secure it. The watching, terrified gathering was a compulsory audience, for any who ran and hid were deemed also to be guilty by the Witchfinder. 'Stand and watch until he is dead,' he had ordered 'and only then may you return to your homes!'

Rachel had been forced to watch that afternoon, staring aghast, biting back her screams as the old man's struggles grew more feeble and his features purpled, his eyes bloated like bubbles about to burst, and bluebottles swarmed and buzzed all over him. Finally he was still, just hanging there. Dead. Everybody had gone home, drifted away, leaving Jason where he was because they dared not move him. Until the morrow. It was a ritual that had to be carried out, and they dared not disobey. Hanging; then gibbetting. At dawn the corvines would come, gouging out the corpse's eyes with their cruel hooked beaks, ribboning the flesh with their talons. Only when the crows had feasted could Jason be buried.

And now the time was nigh for another witchfinding. Any day; any hour. Her eyes became fearful as she continued to keep watch.

Rachel was on the ledge again, but each day now it was more difficult to hope. Travellers passed, and she tensed at each one until she saw that it was not Tabor. She began feeling that her parents and the villagers were right: he would never come. Because he was with whores in London. The thought hurt her deeply, and she pushed it away. She forced herself to believe in him. He had gone south to find his fortune; it had taken longer than he had anticipated, but he would return – to fetch her, to take her to a new life away from this peasant poverty. Faith was difficult, and every night she returned home dejected and tried to close her ears to the taunts of her father. *Oh, Tabor, please come and prove them all wrong.*

With October and the fall of the leaves came the mists, low cloud enshrouding the mountains, sweeping down to cover the moorland. Visibility was reduced to a few yards, and it was likely to remain that way until the gales and rain came to sweep the mist away. She sought the cover of the lone rhododendron bush and huddled amid its damp foliage, her eyes hurting as they tried to penetrate the opaqueness. Hearing oncoming hoofbeats, seeing strangers pass, then groaning her frustration – so it continued. *Please, God, let him come before the winter.*

A sound. She tensed, listening. Not hoofbeats – too light and too slow; a scuffling sound as something was dragged across the stony ground; laboured breathing – she thought it might be human, but surely no human could rasp and wheeze like that and still live.

A shape materialized out of the daytime gloom, a silhouette which she thought was that of a man, tall and stooped, walking with difficulty, unsteadily, twice almost falling. She shrank back into her hiding place; perhaps it was a traveller who had been lost for days up in the mountains, exhausted and starving, in need of help. Or else whoever it was had fallen from his mount and been forced to continue on foot, injured. She moved forward, leaving her hiding place in order to obtain a closer look. He was in full view now, but his head was bent so that she was unable to see his face. He was painfully thin, and his clothing was in tatters so that white wasted flesh was visible in places. He was gasping for breath through tortured lungs, coughing, bent double. Now he was only a few yards away and his head was coming up. That was when she saw his features for the first time – and screamed.

The stranger's face was just patches of flesh amid a scourge of oozing ulcers and weeping sores, thick yellow pus tinged with crimson, congealing as it ran. The eyes were sunk so deep in the black sockets that they might not have existed, and the wide nostrils clogged with dried mucus as they flared and strained for air. The mouth, agape, displayed loose and blackened teeth that wobbled as he fought to breathe. Seeing her, he reached out for her, grunting, and then lapsed back into another spasm of coughing.

Yet in the depths of her revulsion and shock there was recognition, one which she fought against, screamed at. *No, it could not be . . . Tabor. But it was, there was no doubt about it!*

Diseased, festering even as he lived, barely recognizable as the man who had left Garth a few months ago – it was Tabor. Rachel backed off and writhed away from his clutching hands, his pleading grunts. And, still screaming, she fled blindly.

Mercifully the mist swirled in and hid him from her gaze as she looked back just once, and heard his rasping stertorous breathing somewhere behind her. Her reasoning almost snapped, but uppermost was the desire to be away from this creature who was her lover returned.

The inhabitants of Garth were in the entrances to their tumbledown hovels as Rachel ran screaming into the village. All eyes were on her, and the frightened faces of women and children peered out from behind their menfolk, mutely questioning; none dared to ask out loud for they feared what the reply might be. Curious, watching, ready to run back indoors, they guessed perhaps it was the Witchfinder arrived, for his time was nigh – the terrible tall figure dressed in his customary black, his merciless eyes searching for a scapegoat, for he never left a village without a hanging. They looked to one another as they prepared to betray a neighbour or relative. Somebody must die; let it be somebody else.

'What's the matter, wench? What are you wailing for?' It was Rachel's father who spoke gruffly, unkindly.

'It is . . . *Tabor*!' She pointed down the road with a trembling hand.

Heads turned, all eyes stretched into the mist. They heard the wheezing and the dragging of wasted feet before they saw the awful apparition materialize out of the fog.

Twisted cancerous features came into view, the mouth dribbled vile matter as it cursed them incomprehensibly, and bony fists shook feebly at the dwellings on either side of the rough road. It was Tabor, all right, and he had not forgotten his hatred for them whilst he had been away. It had simmered inside him, come to the boil, and seemingly eaten his body away in the process. The living festering entity had the watchers backing indoors, dragging their doors shut and barricading them with any available heavy objects. *Crawl away and die, Tabor, and may the crows and the foxes devour your filthy flesh so that we do not have to look upon it again!*

Two days later the Witchfinder rode into Garth, a spectral form hunched on a scrawny nag. His deep-set eyes flicked from side to side, noting every cottage, seeing the doors barred. He smiled grimly, his thin lips stretched mercilessly across his angular pallid face, as if to say: You cannot hide from me, peasant scum. Come out and determine among yourselves which of you is going to die – and surely one of you will before I leave, for I have yet to find a village where the devil does not dwell in somebody! He sat there waiting, for he was in no hurry. He had learned to savour such occasions; the power over his lesser fellow humans never ceased to delight him. Let them crawl into the open in their own time, he thought, for the longer they waited the more afraid they would be.

A door scraped open and a stocky grimed fellow in

rough clothing showed himself. The Witchfinder read fear in the other's eyes and something else, too – gloating.

'Sir,' Rachel's father spoke humbly in rough rural tones, and bowed his head. 'There is one among us who has the devil in him, is being eaten by evil even as he lives. You must hurry 'ere he dies and the evil spirit inside him leaves and enters one of us.'

'Where is he?' The Witchfinder snapped, tensing, suddenly erect in his saddle. The smile was gone and the small eyes blazed an unholy lust, the expression of a hunter who has cornered his prey.

'In the building at the end of the road.' He jerked his head towards a dilapidated outbuilding with gaping holes in its sagging roof. 'Tabor is bewitched, diseased with a plague caught from whores in London. Nobody will go near him. We have not seen him since he crawled in there. Perchance he is already dead and it is too late.'

'*Fetch him out!*' The Witchfinder snarled.

The peasant paled, stepped back, made as if to dart indoors and drag the door shut, but changed his mind because this horseman was the most feared man in the land. His features drained of colour and he trembled visibly. His mouth opened and the thick lips quivered, but no words came out.

'*Fetch Tabor out*!'

'Yes, sir.'

Doors were being dragged open, men emerging, cowed forms slinking out, watched by their womenfolk and children. The Witchfinder had ordered that Tabor be dragged from his hiding place, and that meant every one of them had to assist – and God help any who hung back.

The Witchfinder sat his horse and watched them trudge fearfully in the direction of the old cowshed then bunch together before the doorway. There was no mistaking their terror, the way they looked at one another, each hoping that the other would enter first. A muttered consultation, then they went forward and peered into the gloomy interior. He heard their gasps of horror, saw them back off and look back at him. Then they squeezed inside, more afraid of the one who sat watching them than of whatever lay within.

A minute, no more, and they emerged, four of them dragging a stinking ulcerated body that was barely recognizable as human. Tabor still lived; at least, his chest rose and fell and slimy bloody mucus bubbled on his mouth and nostrils. His eyes were gone; the corvines might already have ventured in there and feasted. Blind, a dead weight, oblivious to what was happening, the diseased forester hung limply as his arms and legs were lifted off the ground, wheezing faintly. The end could not be far away.

'We are in time.' There was a slight note of relief in the Witchfinder's harsh voice. 'But we must hurry. Get a rope, one of you. The others carry him to the hanging tree.'

One of the younger men broke off and ran to fetch a rope, relieved to be away from that dead-alive body, crossing himself as he went. Heads turned away, the procession carried their burden in the direction of the big tree, which was just visible at the far end of the road, a gaunt gallows constructed by Nature. The Witchfinder kept his distance; for once he did not dismount and approach his victim. His eyes flickered beneath the hooded brows, but there was not one among the company brave enough to look closely and see his expression of fear. Behind him came the women and children, bunched together. Rachel hung back. Her eyes were closed and her fingers clutched her mother's arm. *I don't want to look, I don't want to see. Hang him, and put him out of his misery, whatever it is.*

They were fumbling to slip the noose over Tabor's sagging head, then they tightened it around the near fleshless neck and threw the loose end up over the big bough. Two of them took the strain, their faces averted. Heads turned, they were looking for a sign from the terrible horseman.

The Witchfinder's hand was raised, his head nodded. *Hang him!*

There was a protesting creak from the ancient branch which had borne the weight of a score of executions over the years, and the hempen rope tautened. Those who had been supporting the body leaped away in relief, grateful to be spared further contact. Tabor was dragged upright by his neck. Not so much as a grunt of pain, just a snort of dislodged bloody matter from his clogged nostrils, as he stood, still living, his lungs rattling; then he was borne aloft.

He swung, gyrating first one way then the other. No veins swelled, no eyes bulged out of the dark sockets, just pus pouring from his orifices. The gathering smelled the vile odour and moved back. Even the Witchfinder pulled his mount away.

There was no way of telling whether Tabor was still alive or dead. Arms and feet hung limply, no muscles twitched. The peasants had grouped and were awaiting a sign that they had permission to leave – and praying God that the crows and hawks did a good job before the burying tomorrow!

'Cut him down!'

Heads jerked round at the command, and there were muttered grunts of horrified surprise. *No, please, not yet!*

It might have been an optical illusion, but the Witchfinder's lips appeared to tremble as he spoke. 'I said cut him down and bury him. The evil in that body lives on and nothing will destroy it. When it has devoured every morsel of diseased flesh on those bones it will move on in search of another body. The only way to be sure is to bury the corpse so deep that the undying plague cannot find a way out.'

A rippled gasp of terror greeted his words.

'You heard me.' The black-clad man was already wheeling his mount and there was no mistaking his urgency to leave. 'Tabor has a plague the likes of which I have only heard whispered, one that devours body and *soul*, and then, still hungering, goes in search of further prey. There is still time, there is still flesh left on his body, but do not delay. Inter him as deep as the well from which you draw your water, for your own safety. And may the good Lord protect you from that which they call the Festering!'

He wheeled his horse, dug his heels into its flanks, and within minutes the Witchfinder was swallowed up by the late afternoon fog as it began to roll back towards the village.

A dozen frightened men went to fetch spades and buckets and ropes with which to haul the surplus soil out of the deep shaft. There was still a couple of hours of foggy daylight left, and they wasted no time in setting to work. Earth was thrown to one side, causing miniature avalanches as the mound grew. The hole was deepening; now two men were waist-deep in it, shovelling frantically, then up to their necks; soon a ladder would be necessary.

The womenfolk stood back, watching; there was nothing they could do to help, but they were afraid to return to their empty houses. The Witchfinder's warning still echoed in their ears. *The Festering*.

Tabor's body hung from the bough, and those brave enough to look saw how that stinking dribble still oozed and dried on the wasted frame, an entity that lived even though the flesh was dead, seeping out as if it already hungered for another. They would leave it there until they were ready for it; let the scavenging birds enjoy a diseased repast.

Only darkness halted their progress and sent them back to their hovels, where they skulked fearfully throughout a sleepless night. Soon after first light they returned to their work. Tabor still dangled from his gallows, now unrecognizable beneath a layer of caked cancerous matter, a waxen figure awaiting its burial patiently. Another day's work, and still the diggers were not finished; another night of terror, but by midday on the third day the shaft was mutually agreed to be deep enough. In frantic haste, the corpse was cut down and dragged by its rope to the top of the hole, where a long pole was used to topple it over the edge.

In silence they listened; if they had been other than uneducated peasants they would have counted the seconds. As it was they just waited; time seemed to have stopped. Then they sighed their relief as they heard a muffled thud from far below.

Even the women joined their men in a frenzy to shovel back the excavated soil, working with their hands because there were not enough shovels. They were finished just as darkness closed in like a God-sent mantle to hide this time of terror. And afterwards they knelt and prayed that they had been in time.

That the Festering was destroyed for ever.

1

'I could live here forever.' There was a note of ecstasy in Holly Mannion's voice as she gazed back from the overgrown garden at the small stone cottage with ivy and virginia creeper competing for space over the crumbling stonework. Window sills had rotted over the last couple of decades, some slates were missing from the roof, a downspout was clinging on by a single bracket; dereliction, but right now in the warm summer sunlight Garth Cottage was the most beautiful place on earth.

There was a smile on Holly's soft lips, her dark eyes shone and her slim fingers brushed away a strand of long black hair which the warm breeze had wafted over her finely cut features. Shorts and a bikini top showed off her shapely figure to perfection. Feeling carefree, she spoke her thoughts aloud. Because it felt good being out here, miles away from the town and the nine-to-five routine which had dominated their lives for the last six years. She knew now what 'getting away from it all' felt like: it was a sense of freedom. You didn't give a damn so long as you had something to eat and a roof over your head, even if there were slates missing, the rafters had warped and on wet nights rain dripped through into the only bedroom. Right now it was hot and the sun shone and nothing else mattered.

'It won't be so good in winter.' The tall bearded man did not glance up from where he stood endeavouring to point up a wide crack between the stones in the wall, pursing his lips as he filled the uneven narrow gully with cement which was drying out too fast in the warmth. He tried not to think about the half-finished landscape which rested on the easel in his improvised lean-to-studio. The trouble with this new lifestyle, he concluded, was that there were too many distractions. If he remained indoors working on his painting, then he felt he ought to be outside making the most of this unprecedented heat-wave; and when he succumbed to that temptation and struggled to master the art of pointing, he felt guilty because he should be working. Whichever way he looked at it, he couldn't win. A chunk of half-dried cement crumbled and fell out of the hole. Mike Mannion grunted his annoyance, dropped his trowel and turned round.

'Grumpy!' his wife taunted him. 'Just because you can't get the cement to stay in place doesn't mean that life is going to be all drudgery here, Mike. We'll get by, one way or another. After all, I can't expect to have a husband who's a brickie as well as a talented artist, can I?'

'No.' A half-smile touched his bearded lips. 'But you knew that before you married me. Damn it, I can't even knock a nail in straight, so how the hell can we expect to renovate this place without either the know-how or the money? We don't have either. At the moment we're just breaking even, and I just hope to God I sell that picture which I should be finishing instead of wasting my time on a patching up job that won't be any good when I've finished it, anyway. You might well change your mind about living out here when winter comes.'

It had been Holly's idea to pack up and leave their home in the Midlands. Mike had been quite content living in a terraced house, where he had his small studio in the second bedroom. There was little gardening required of him, gas central heating which was reasonably economic and few other overheads. And when his pictures weren't selling, there was always Holly's monthly secretarial salary to fall back upon. All an artist asked of life was the tools of his trade and somewhere to work. But Holly had been bitten by this get-out-of-the-rat-race bug, just as their friends Dave and Moira had been. Mike reckoned that they had influenced his wife, brainwashed her into the idea. Dave had been a bank clerk with reasonable prospects, but he had thrown them all overboard for a five-acre smallholding that was mostly Welsh mountain scrubland and would just about support a few sheep and some hens. Back to the good life, and to hell with it if they faced near poverty. 'Freedom' was the word they had used; nobody to tell you what you had to do as your stomach rumbled and you consulted that book about food from the hedgerows.

Mike had resisted the idea, but once Holly's mind was made up, he knew he might as well save his breath. Their town house had sold miraculously quickly – he had hoped secretly that there would be no takers and in due course Holly would abandon her wild scheme. They had made fifteen hundred pounds profit after they had bought Garth Cottage and its one and a half acres of wilderness, but that money had been swallowed up on the basic improvements needed to make it habitable and the addition of his studio. He still wondered if they should have obtained planning permission for it, but the farmer who had sold them the cottage assured them that it wasn't necessary and, in any case, out here the planning people didn't give a cuss what you did. Mike hoped that nobody from the council would come out to check.

Anyway, what was done was done. They were living right out in the sticks in a tumbledown stone dwelling, which the estate agent had assured them had 'potential', and it was no good moaning. If Mike's agent managed to sell his latest picture, then at least they would have a little cash in hand. Otherwise . . . he grimaced. Life out here could be a lot tougher than in the town if the dice were loaded against you.

'I'll go and make a cup of tea.' Holly sensed his mood but she wasn't relenting. 'Comfrey or raspberry leaf? Or chamomile?'

'Just a plain old ordinary tea bag, thanks,' he retorted.

'Please yourself.' She began to walk towards the cottage, biting back the remark on the tip of her tongue that if the picture didn't sell, then it was going to be herb tea fresh from the hedgerows from then on, whether he liked it or not. This was not the time to remind him of that; maybe tomorrow he would go back to his painting and then she would take over the pointing; DIY was more her line than her husband's. Much more.

Mike scooped up another lump of cement on his trowel and studied it pensively. The mix was too dry, that was why it was falling out all the time. Make it too sloppy, and it just trickled out of the crack. There had to be a happy medium; he would try just one more time. He reached out for the watering can, but knew by its lightness even as he lifted it up that it was empty. Damn it, everything was against him today, he sighed. He would go into the kitchen and fill it at the sink, and stop for a cup of tea, herb or conventional brew, whilst he was there. And afterwards. . . .

'Mike!' There was consternation on Holly's face as she met him at the door, the same expression as when she had discovered that the floorboards in the bedroom had dry rot, and again when she first became aware of the rising damp in the kitchen. He groaned inwardly.

'Let's have that cup of tea before you tell me.' Somehow he managed to grin.

'We can't.' Now there was genuine despair in her voice, a tone of helplessness. 'Mike, there's nothing coming out of the taps. We're out of water!'

His initial reaction was to exclaim in relieved tones, 'Well, that puts paid to my pointing. Now I can go and finish that picture.' Slowly the implications of a waterless existence filtered through to him; his mouth was suddenly dry and it was difficult to swallow. No tea, for a start; nothing to drink at all unless they carried water from the brook a quarter of a mile away and boiled it; no flushing the loo, washing up, bathing, or a dozen things that you took for granted in the town. He leaned up against the doorpost, took a deep breath and let it out slowly. 'Let me have a try.' His words lacked conviction as he crossed to the old stone sink.

He was hoping that by some miracle water would gush out of the taps if he turned them on hard enough. Aware of his wife's scathing expression, he wrenched at the taps and eventually managed a few drips into the washing-up bowl. That was all; and after a few moments even the dripping stopped.

'Mike, whatever are we going to do?'

He did not reply. Instead his impracticable mind was trying to recall the mechanics of their water system, which the taciturn Hughes had shown them the day they had looked over Garth Cottage. A botch-up of a system, a Heath Robinson effort devised by the old farmer primarily to run water to the old cottage at minimum expense so that it could be put on the open market. A hydraulic ram was situated in a bricked-up well somewhere in the stream about three-quarters of a mile away, a complicated-looking contraption that worked on pressure and did so many thumps to the minute, and pumped up one gallon of water for every ten that it let swirl on downstream. The thing was roofed with a piece of rusted corrugated tin sheeting with holes in it. Somehow the water went uphill through some PVC piping that was buried in an old forestry furrow, all the way to the top, where it crossed the lane through a council land drain. It went on another two hundred yards, serving a couple of sheep drinking troughs, until it finally flowed weakly into a small five-hundred-gallon reservoir, which it filled up to the outlet pipe, and trickled on down to supply the cottage.

' 'E kept goin' all through that summer of seventy-six,' Hughes had commented slyly, refraining from mentioning that at the time of that historic drought nobody had been living at Garth Cottage; in all probability the reservoir had not been built then, and all the ram had to supply was a couple of troughs to satisfy a few thirsty hill sheep.

'We'd better go and have a look in the reservoir.' Mike slipped an arm around Holly's slim waist. One step at a time he thought. Of course, the reservoir would be empty – that was a foregone conclusion – but it seemed a positive move. Then they would trek down to the lower forest and wade up the stream until they came to the ram, and see if it was working. It probably wasn't. In which case the buck had to be passed to Elwyn Hughes. His enthusiasm towards the Mannions seemed to have waned somewhat since the completion of the sale. All the same, there was a clause in the deeds that he had to supply them with domestic water. Mike's lips tightened; he'd damned well make that miserly old hill farmer get the water flowing again. If you did not have the know-how yourself, you had to resort to other means. He clenched his fists until his knuckles whitened.

The reservoir was empty, as Mike had anticipated. He knew by the hollow sound which the heavy concrete hatch made when he dropped it as he struggled to lift it up, a booming echo from within like a controlled underground explosion. They stared into the gloomy tomb-like depths and saw the half-inch or so of water on the floor below. Some water beetles were swimming in it, and there was a spider's web halfway down the far wall, the water had not been flowing in here for a week at least.

'So much for that.' Mike let the heavy cover drop back, detonating another miniature earthquake beneath them, and felt the vibrations escalating his sense of futility. The ram wasn't working, for sure, but they would go and look, all the same.

The forest was cool and shady after the heat of the slope above – forbidding, in a way, Holly thought, like those dark woods in childhood fairytale books that harboured ogres and evil dwarfs. Trees with twisted holes became leering faces if you looked at them long enough. She clasped Mike's hand tightly and told herself not to be so stupid; their worry was their water supply, not imagined bogeymen.

In places, they had to duck down beneath low branches and fight their way through bramble bushes and clumps of pink wild willow herb. She was sweating, but felt relieved when at last they reached the narrow sluggish stream. There was only an inch or so of water in it; it had narrowed to a channel barely six inches wide, and the mud on either side was caked and cracking. Her hopes were falling fast, and she was reminded of that tiny terraced house where there was always water in the taps, even if it was laced with chlorine and fluoride and any other nasties which the bureaucratic water board chose to contaminate it with. At least it was wet and plentiful, even if it made the strongest cup of tea taste of chemicals. No, that was no way to be thinking. Sod the water authorities, she would prefer to collect her own unpalatable drinking water out of the stream with a bucket than be subjected to their unthinkable harmful additives. She had her principles, which was why she and Mike had moved out to the Garth.

A square of chipped and crumbling brickwork rose up out of the shallow watercourse up ahead of them like some gremlin's dwelling place. She tensed as Mike stopped, aware of his breathing in the still atmosphere. A moment of fleeting panic, then she knew that he had only stopped to listen, straining his ears to catch the *thump-thump-thump* of the ram like some mechanical heartbeat building up to a crescendo. Hoping, they desperately willed their ears to pick up the rhythmic vibrations. But there was only silence.

They did not speak as they moved forward, Mike dropping to a crouch as he struggled to lift off the rusted cover weighed down with stones, which he sent splashing into the feeble current.

They both stared at the ugly cast-iron monstrosity that stood lifeless in its brick prison, the deformed dwarf of Holly's imagined fears earlier, sombre black streaked with red rust, a statuette condemned to a watery grave, a victim of Man's mechanical ingenuity that had died and still stood upright. Half an inch of water swirled around its base then went its way unmolested.

'The ram's stopped: that's why we've got no water.' Mike voiced the obvious because one of them had to say something about the confirmation of their fears. They stared, foolishly praying that suddenly this lifeless piece of mechanism would start to pump again. But it wouldn't.

'I wonder how it works.' Mike Mannion leaned forward, touched it and felt the icy coldness of a dead thing, an iron corpse.

'However it works, you won't get it going again!' There was sarcasm in Holly's voice, a tone she immediately regretted. She was being unfair to her husband. Unless you understood hydraulic water machines you didn't stand an earthly of maintaining them. She was being unfair to him. 'I'm sorry,' she whispered, and squeezed his arm. She wasn't going to ask him what he was going to do next. They had both run out of ideas, and right now she felt an urge to burst into tears. She wondered if she would feel better if she did, releasing her pent-up frustrations.

'I think I'll have a word with old Hughes.' He straightened up, and she heard his knee joints cracking as if he had stepped on some dry twigs. 'We'll walk back that way. Damn the fellow, he can get down here and get it going again.'

The old hill farmer regarded them stoically across the rusted gate which separated his yard from the track leading up from the lane below, a kind of dilapidated barrier erected to keep out townies who chose to infiltrate the wild lands of his forefathers. Small and wizened, he wore the same tattered brown shepherd's smock that had seen him through last winter. He pursed his lips pensively. It was impossible even to guess his innermost thoughts, but Holly decided that, one way or the other, he did not intend to help them. He had sold them the cottage; they had their dwelling, he had his money and that was that. Whatever was written into the title deeds was just words on a piece of paper; this wasn't the town – out here life was different. Furthermore, the Mannions were outsiders and that was Elwyn Hughes' criterion in this case.

'We're out of water,' Mike said for the third time. 'The ram has stopped working.'

The farmer regarded them steadily. Not so much as a flicker of those grey eyes, just a pursing of the lips, a dribble of saliva as he sucked on his dead pipe. 'It's the drought.' He spoke softly, almost menacingly. 'If you'm don't have rain, you'm don't have water.'

'I am well aware of that fact.' Mike's tone was clipped. 'It's not the drought I'm talking about, it's the *ram*. It's stopped. It . . . isn't . . . working!' *Christ, doesn't he understand?*

'That's what I'm tellin' you.' There was a slight note of irritation in the farmer's voice now. 'The ram's stopped because there isn't any rain. The water level in yon stream has dropped; there isn't enough water to make the ram work. Now d'you understand, Mr Mannion?'

Mike felt his stomach contract and suddenly the day did not seem so warm. With a sudden chill he realized they did not have any water because the ram had stopped, and the ram had stopped because there wasn't any water. Catch 22, as the saying went.

'Do you understand what I'm saying, Mr Mannion? There's no water so — '

'Yes,' Mike answered slowly. 'I understand.'

'But what are we going to do?' Holly thought her voice sounded shrill, as though it bordered on hysteria. 'Can't you *make* it work, Mr Hughes?'

'No.' Those wizened lips parted in a smile which might have been sadistic delight, and the head moved slowly from side to side. 'Only the good Lord can get it going again, Mrs Mannion, and He'll do that when He's ready. In His own good time. Now, do you understand?'

She said 'yes' meekly and hated herself for it, then added, 'but isn't there *anything* we can do?'

The farmer pondered, taking his time replying, almost as though he was debating whether or not to advise these outsiders further. 'You'm could get yourself a borehole,' he said at length.

'A *borehole*?' Mike stared in amazement. 'What the devil is a borehole?'

'A well.' Hughes spoke condescendingly as if he was addressing an infant class in a village school. 'There's a good many folks havin' 'em drilled nowadays, mostly them that have moved out here from the towns.' He paused to let the implication register. 'No trouble. Bennions are doin' 'em as fast as they can get the rig from one place to the other. Take a tip from me and get yourselves a borehole.'

And let *you* off the hook, Mike thought, and clenched his fists angrily. You'll have all the water you want for your stock then. He said, 'It's an idea, certainly. We'd have *two* water supplies then, a well *and* the ram, Mr Hughes!'

The old man's eyes narrowd, his thin lips tightened, and then, without another word, he turned away and shuffled back into the farmyard.

'Well,' Mike shrugged, 'we don't appear to have any choice, Holly. It's either a borehole or going without water. We'd better have a look in the phone book and see where these Bennion folk hang out. I get the feeling I'm going to have to get that painting finished and sold pretty quick!'

2

Mike Mannion was pleasantly surprised by his first impression of Frank Bennion. He had anticipated a rough, overall-clad figure smeared with tractor grease, possibly another antagonist of 'outsiders'. Instead, the managing director of F. Bennion & Co. Ltd. was smartly dressed in a tweed suit, spotless shirt and tie, with clean wellingtons on his feet and a clipboard tucked under his arm.

'Mr Mannion?' The visitor extended a hand, a smile on his fresh clean-shaven face.

'You'd better come inside, Mr Bennion.' Mike held the door wide, sensed Holly behind him.

'First things, first.' Bennion glanced behind him at the overgrown patch of garden surrounding the cottage. 'Before we waste each other's time, I think we'd better ascertain that there actually is water here, don't you think?' Another smile. 'I expect you've seen the guarantee with our newspaper advertisements. "No water, no fee". You can't be fairer than that, can you? Most of the drilling firms nowadays don't guarantee you water. They want a couple of grand off you before they start to drill, and if there's no water down there then it costs you another five hundred to get the shaft filled in. *We* guarantee water, or if we don't find any then it doesn't cost you a penny.'

'I see.' Mike found himself following the other man round the house, Bennion walking fast, confidently, then stopping, looking round as if he was trying to get his bearings.

'I think we'll start here. Just hold my clipboard for me, will you, Mr Mannion?' Bennion was delving in his pocket, searching amid coins that rattled, and eventually pulled out a length of string with a polished wooden conical-shaped object attached to the end. He let it dangle and spin, caressing it almost lovingly. 'Do you know anything about pendulums, Mr Mannion?'

'Er . . . no.' Mike shifted, felt embarrassed and glanced at Holly. 'I'm afraid I don't.'

'Never mind.' Bennion was holding the end of the string between thumb and forefinger, steadying the spinning weight with his other hand, releasing it when it was still. 'More reliable than copper wands, at least, as far as I'm concerned. When it finds water it'll spin clockwise, anticlockwise if there isn't any. Just watch, please, I have to concentrate.'

Mike and Holly watched, fascinated; at first the pendulum did not move, then, with some hesitancy, it began to swing in an anticlockwise direction. Bennion grunted and moved on a few yards. The same ritual; the pendulum told him for the second time that there was no water directly beneath where he stood. On again, a full ten yards this time, standing in a slight hollow covered with sun-scorched weeds.

'Ah!' There was satisfaction in his exclamation, and his grey eyes were shining with boyish delight. 'I think we may be in luck this time.'

The pendulum swung in a clockwise arc, then made a full circle, gathering momentum all the time until Frank Bennion snatched it back and dropped it into his pocket. 'There's water down here, and plenty of it by the pull. I don't think we'll need to look elsewhere. This is an ideal spot for the borehole, far enough from the house so that it doesn't get sprayed with slurry when we drill. Now, perhaps we could go indoors and I'll put a few figures down on paper so that you'll know what you're in for. No offence if you turn us down, Mr Mannion.' He laughed good-humouredly.

Mike experienced a fluttering in his stomach. He had no idea what all this would cost – a thousand pounds for sure. He asked, 'How long will the job take?' A good guideline to the financial aspect, he thought, and held his breath. He reminded himself that Daniels, his agent, was expecting an offer any day on that painting he had only finished last week.

'A couple of days, three at the most.' Bennion seated himself down at the scrubbed pine table and began jotting some figures on an estimate sheet.

'Coffee, Mr Bennion?' Mike noted the slight tension in

Holly's voice; she was apprehensive too. They had not budgeted for the outlay on a water system. That was hitch number one. How many more were hidden in this new lifestyle waiting to pounce?

'Thank you, Mrs Mannion.' Bennion answered without glancing up, scribbled something on the paper and sucked the end of his ballpoint.

Mike was watching Bennion closely. He might have been mistaken for a gentleman farmer, an astute agriculturist who had made his pile. Well-spoken, affluent; that was a BMW parked out in the lane, and at a glance the car looked new. Bennion was surely of retirement age, possibly over it, the kind who never stopped working and dropped down still wearing his green wellies when his time was up. He sipped his coffee without taking his eyes off the paper in front of him, furrowing his forehead as he made mental calculations, then wrote something else.

For Frank Bennion life was idyllic. He remembered 'the old days' with nostalgia – the time when he had been just an ordinary agricultural contractor. In the spring he'd contracted for as much ploughing as he could get, followed by corn sowing. Harvest time had been the worst because it was dependent upon the weather; a fine spell after a wet one, and everybody thought you ought to cut their corn first. Hedging in the autumn – pleaching in those days, not this unsightly foliage-gobbling with a mechanical flail that tore indiscriminately at everything in its patch and left a mile of hawthorn looking as if some ravenous browsing monster had feasted along it. Hard work then, and the money wasn't good because he'd had to undercut his competitors to get any work at all.

Then Frank had invested in a second-hand quarry rig and begun drilling water wells as a sideline. In the beginning it was just the odd one, then this craze began where folks moved out from the towns to a new lifestyle – they called it 'self-sufficiency', but it was all a game; they expected the mod cons to go with it. These newcomers to the countryside weren't prepared to fetch their water from the stream or do without when their shallow well ran dry. So the boom in boreholes began, and Frank found it more profitable than ploughing and hedge-trimming. He took on a youth to do the labouring, then a man to work the rig; finally an electrician and a plumber so that they could do the whole job from start to finish. He had drilled six hundred wells to date; the Mannions would be number six hundred and one. If they accepted the estimate.

He paused and took another sip of coffee. 'Will you be wanting to use your own plumber, Mr Mannion?'

'Er . . . not really.' Mike did not even know a plumber in the area.

'I see. Then I'll quote you for plumbing as well.' Bennion was writing again.

Mike shifted uncomfortably in his chair and looked across at Holly. She was pale, uneasy. But they did not have to accept the quote; they could simply wait for the rains to come. But from this morning's forecast on the radio, that might be a long time. The weathermen were already talking about another 1976.

'I think that's about it.' There was a sense of smug satisfaction about Bennion as he pushed the sheet of paper across the table to Mike. Mike picked it up and found himself reading it line by line, the fingers holding it shaking slightly. It read:

ESTIMATE FOR WATER-WELL

60′ bore-hole, with well casing, seal from surface contamination & cap with pit & manhole	£850.00
Extra footage @ £7.50 per ft. if needed	
Pump & controls	320.00
Cable in bore	40.00
Cable to bore	35.00
Probes	80.00

Weatherproof control box	20.00
External electrics	45.00
Float & pilot cable	26.00
Rising main in bore	30.00
Delivery pipe from bore	24.00
Fitting & control valves	18.00
Excavation of trench to dwelling	60.00
Labour and journeys	220.00
Interior plumbing	200.00
Total	£1,970.00

'It may be more . . . or less,' Bennion added softly, 'depending upon whether we need to drill deeper than sixty feet. I hope that won't be necessary.'

Mike's vision swam. The figures in front of him merged, swirling like a still pond into which a pebble had been tossed. Holly was trying to read the estimate from the end of the table but was too polite to lean across. *Jesus Christ, close on two grand!*

'When would you be thinking of starting, Mr Bennion?' The question seemed to come out casually, but he hoped the older man could not hear the pounding of his pulses or detect a quaver in his voice. Knowing contractors, it might be weeks, months – in which case the rains would probably have come by then. Then they could cancel.

'Let me see.' Frank Bennion pulled a diary out of his pocket and flicked some pages. 'Today's Monday. Say Wednesday, Thursday at the latest.'

'*This* week!'

'Surely. We're just finishing off at that white-washed cottage that stands up on the hillside as you come into Garth. A mile away – less, probably. It's very convenient for moving the tack here. If we had to travel from home it would cost you a fair bit more. It's cheap, Mr Mannion.'

Waiting for an answer, drumming a finger on the table, Bennion thought, hurry up, Mr Mannion, I've got three more estimates to do before lunch.

'I. . . .' Just at that second the phone shrilled; it seemed to scream a warning: Don't take it, Mike, you can't afford it. You'll be in debt for years if you do.

'I'll get it.' There was relief in Holly's voice as she leaped up and almost ran to the wall phone by the Welsh dresser. Mike sucked in his breath. A welcome interlude; breathing space; a few seconds during which he could still hang on to that two thousand he didn't have.

'For you, Mike.' Holly was holding out the receiver, leaning against the wall with her free hand. 'It's Bob Daniels.'

'Excuse me a moment.' Mike returned their visitor's fixed smile. 'I won't be a moment.'

'Mike.' The art agent sounded continents away, his voice lower than usual as if he spoke in confidence and was afraid of being overheard in his own office. 'The picture – I've had an offer.'

'How much?' The all-important question. *Tell me it's two grand because I'm going to spend it in about ten seconds flat.*

'Not just *the* picture, Mike. That and others. Dowsons, the commercial art publishers, are interested in a series of similar landscapes to do limited-edition prints. They want a contract for ten!'

'I see.' If Bennion had not been less than six feet away Mike might have said 'Holy Christ Almighty!' His pulse rate speeded up still further and he mouthed into the handset, 'What's the deal, then, Bob?'

'Ten grand. Five on signature, a thousand on delivery of each painting. I know you'll accept. I already have on your behalf.'

Mike caught his breath. He did not trust himself to speak. If Bennion guessed, then there might be a few extras on that estimate. 'That's marvellous. Go ahead, Bob, and I'll call you back in a bit. Okay?'

'Sure.' The agent sounded disappointed. Maybe he got his kicks from hearing whoops of joy from his clients, Mike thought as he replaced the receiver, barely trusting himself to walk back to the table. Bennion was already on his feet, his clipboard under his arm ready for his next customer, and picking up his floppy hat.

'I'll have to be on my way, Mr Mannion.' He was still smiling, but it seemed forced now, irritated, disappointed. Time was money, and these people had wasted an hour of his time.

'We'll see you Thursday. Or Friday at the latest.' Mike derived a kind of pleasure from the casual way he spoke.

'Oh . . . fine.' Bennion's former smile returned. 'You can rely on us, Mr Mannion. We'll find you water. And if we don't, then you won't owe us a penny.' And then he was gone through the door, striding down the weed-covered path, the jauntiness back in his step.

'Mike!' Holly's features were white and she was trembling, half-angry. 'You know we can't afford that sort of — '

'We can . . . now.' He pulled her to him and kissed her quivering lips. 'I almost think Bob Daniels is telepathic. Or something. He's sold that picture, and nine more to go with them. Our only worry right now is what Frank Bennion finds at the bottom of the well he's going to drill. Water, I hope!'

3

Holly had not really expected drilling to commence on Thursday. Or Friday. Contractors were all the same: promises, excuses, delays – it would be two to three weeks before they turned up, and only then after repeated reminders. Consequently she was surprised when just after ten o'clock on Thursday morning a battered old long-wheel-base Land Rover arrived towing the rig, followed by an ex-WD lorry which had been converted into a mobile compressor. A fresh-faced youth and an older, stocky, taciturn man in torn overalls busied themselves backing the rig through the front gate and down to that shallow dip in the weedy garden where water had been divined. She looked for Bennion, but there was no sign of the dapper boss; his job ended with dowsing and writing out the estimate probably.

She stood there on the step, watching them unhitch the rig, and had numerous misgivings about the wisdom of the enterprise. A large proportion of Mike's advance on the paintings was invested in it – or, rather, it would be when the cheque arrived. She just hoped there were no hitches, no second thoughts by the art publishers. Frank Bennion did not look the kind of man who would wait patiently for his money.

'Here we go, then.' Mike appeared from the kitchen. 'Bang on time. It's a good job we hadn't made a start on the garden. God knows what kind of a mess they'll leave behind when they've done.'

The two workmen laboured frantically, cursing beneath their breath as they endeavoured to connect up all the various machinery. The compressor was parked in the gateway; Mike wondered how he was expected to get his car out, but he would meet that problem if the need arose. Large metal drums were unloaded from the back of the Land Rover and linked up like undisciplined soldiers; then coils of rope, a length of cable, spades, numerous bags of sand and gravel. The two men might have been oblivious of their audience for all the notice they took. There was an almost frantic haste about their movements.

'I reckon Bennion must be a slave-driver, the way those blokes are running about,' Mike mused. 'They've probably got so many boreholes to drill that they don't know which way to turn. Anyway, I can't stand here all day watching them, I've got to get cracking with the next landscape. See you at coffee time, darling.' He gave her a pouted kiss on the back of her neck and walked across to his improvised studio.

Hardly had Mike begun to paint before the flimsy studio floor was vibrating, as a noise like a nearby road drill escalated by the second, building up to a deafening peak then maintaining its drone. Everything shook. The easel was probably rattling, but it was impossible to hear it above the din; Mike's hand shook so that he changed his mind and replaced the brush on the tray. Damn it, he thought, he couldn't paint in *this*, he couldn't hold a paintbrush steady, let alone concentrate. The floor seemed to be heaving up, rising another six inches and shaking, and the door swung open on its rickety catch. Mike closed the paint tray and sat looking at it. Two days, maybe three, in which work was impossible. He thought about going into the house and trying to paint there. No, it would not be any better indoors. He sighed, then moved to the doorway to watch, because there wasn't anything else to do.

Jesus Christ Almighty! The untended garden bore no resemblance to the one he had viewed a few minutes earlier. From the elevated mouth of the rig a stream of thick grey oily slurry spouted high into the air. The jet arced, fell on the topmost boughs of a japonica tree, dripped from the branches and oozed its way down the trunk. Then it spread out into a thickening, widening pool, following the fall of the land, covering everything in its path as it crept relentlessly across the ground. Six feet from the front door, it had already determined its course, sliming towards the overgrown shrubbery. Sludge, mud and filth, and judging by its shiny texture – which reminded Mike of early morning snail tracks on the broken patio outside the back door – there was some kind of chemical mixed with it. The compressor in the gateway roared its approval at the mess the rig was creating, and seemed to increase its volume. The fountain of underground waste was unending. Gone was the green foliage of summer, and in its place was colourless, unrecognizable vegetation, a morass that dripped and spread – moving desecration. He half-wondered if it was safe to cross the drive to the cottage. Don't be bloody stupid, it's only liquid mud, he told himself. *But is it?* He shuddered, and had to resist the temptation to make a dash for it. Walking quickly all the same, he tried not to look. It gave him the creeps and . . . *oh, my Christ, what a smell!*

The odour seared the back of his throat. It was like walking into some vile-smelling swamp fog, except that it was far worse. The lingering, penetrating stench made him heave and want to throw up. Too late to take a deep breath and hold it; he coughed, gagged and experienced an urge to vomit. Then he was at the door, opening it quickly and slamming it shut behind him, gulping down the faint cooking smells which wafted through from the kitchen.

'Are you all right, Mike?' Holly stood by the Rayburn, stirring something in a saucepan. There was genuine alarm on her face.

'I'm okay,' he smiled wanly, 'apart from the noise and the smell.'

'I've shut all the windows to try and keep that dreadful stink out of the house.' She wrinkled her nose. 'But there's nothing that will stop that awful din from getting in. Maybe we should go out, keep away until they've finished.'

'Maybe.' He went to the sink and began washing his hands in some leftover washing-up water. Except that we're trapped, he thought, because I can't get the car out and I'll only prolong the job if I ask them to switch the compressor off and move the truck.

'I can't imagine what's making that stench,' she went on. 'After all, they're only drilling through rock and soil. I hope to God there isn't some foul bog down there. We've got to drink the water that comes up out of it!'

'Bennion guaranteed us water, didn't he?' Defiantly, he challenged that three-day-old promise.

'But he didn't promise us *pure* water, did he?' Holly's expression was strained with the thought that had been nagging her.

'Surely that's what he means.' Mike's words lacked conviction.

'We'll have to see what the final product is like.' Holly realized there was no point in getting worked up at this stage. 'I thought all country cottages had sparkling crystal clear water.'

'Maybe we will.' Mike dried his hands, idly wondering how they were going to pass the rest of today. And tomorrow. And the day after. 'Anyway, as soon as there's water coming out of the taps, I'm going to ask the Environmental Health Department to test it. I promise you one thing, Holly, Bennion doesn't get a penny of his money until the water is passed fit to drink.'

'Surely the drilling won't take all day,' she resisted the temptation to look out of the window at that moving, stinking swamp. 'Sixty feet is what Bennion said they should find water at, and the rate that drill's going they can't be far off now.'

Three hours later the rig was still jetting its foul residue over the japonica tree. Mike felt a headache coming on; this afternoon he and Holly would go for a long walk, he decided, right through the village and out as far as the Bryn. And they wouldn't hurry back. Tomorrow they would find somewhere else to walk; if he couldn't work, then he might as well make the most of the summer weather away from all this.

Without warning, the compressor cut out, clanked to a halt, bringing a stillness that was in some ways as frightening as the noise itself. Mike was aware in those few seconds just how much his head throbbed and his nerves shook. He had a fleeting urge to scream, just looking at Holly, bracing himself for the return of the vibrations. But the silence continued.

‘I expect they’ve knocked off for lunch.’ Holly was the first to speak; she discovered that she was shouting, then whispering. ‘Or else they’ve finished,’ But she didn’t want to go out there to ask them. She preferred to stay indoors, where they were safe.

‘Let’s eat and then. . . .’

A sudden knocking on the door interrupted Mike, and made him start. The noise reverberated in the small room, and was frightening for a second. Then he laughed, a hollow, forced sound. ‘I expect it’s one of the workmen.’

It was the youth, his overalls shiny with that mud glistening evilly in the bright sunlight. In his hand he had a polythene water carrier. ‘Excuse me, chief,’ he grinned. ‘Can we ’ave some water to make the tea?’

‘Water!’ It was Mike’s turn to laugh. ‘We don’t have any water, mate. That’s why you’re drilling for it out there.’

‘Oh!’ A moment’s perlexity, then, ‘Didn’t realize you didn’t ’ave none at all. Anywhere ’andy we can get some?’

‘You’ll have to walk down into the village. There’s an outside tap on the garage forecourt.’

The younger man pulled a face and drummed the container in his dilemma; he didn’t care for walking – operating heavy machinery was more his scene. ‘Guess we’ll ’ave to walk to the village, then. My mate’ll go.’

‘What’s that awful stink out there?’ Mike was easing the door closed. The stench was drifting in as if it had been lurking out there for hours awaiting its opportunity to invade the cottage. ‘What the hell is it?’

‘Christ knows!’ A grimace and a shrug of the shoulders. ‘Never smelled ’owt like it before, chief. Like sommat’s rottin’ down there. You ain’t got your septic tank there, ’ave you?’ His laugh seemed to have got strangled between his throat and his lips.

Mike Mannion felt cold fingers twisting his intestines, compressing them into a hard ball. This fellow was admitting that he had never smelled anything like it before, and he had drilled six hundred boreholes!

'It's gotta be sommat in the ground,' the youth mumbled.

'Like what?'

'Search me. Maybe there's a soak hole down there, and all the dung from one of the farms drains into it.'

'Jesus! Then in that case you'd better fill it all in and forget the well. We have to drink the water, you know.'

'Aw, it won't be as bad as that. If it is a soak hole, then it'll only be close to the surface. Deep down the water's always pure. If it's surface contamination then it's easily sealed off. Don't you worry 'bout that, we've come across scores of surface pollution and we've always got pure water from beneath it. A metre of soil is enough to filter water.'

Mike sighed his relief aloud and closed the door as the youth returned to the Land Rover, where his stocky companion was immersed in a tabloid daily. A hiccup, nothing more; the onus was on F. Bennion & Co. Ltd. to rectify the problem. It's not our worry, he reassured himself. Except that we have to put up with that stink in the meantime.

'Damn it.' He turned to Holly.' I never asked him how deep they've drilled so far. Well, I'm not going back out there. Come on, let's have something to eat, and then we'll leave them to it for an hour or two.'

The Bryn, with its rolling grassy slopes, reminded Holly Mannion of underdone breakfast toast; the heatwave had already begun to take its toll of the wiry hill grass, turning it into growing hay, and the sheep were sheltering from the direct rays of the sun in the patches of gorse and bracken. The dry heat was pleasant in comparison with the humidity of the usual British summer. Unless you were a farmer. Or a fireman, she realized. One carelessly dropped cigarette end could start a raging inferno in these brittle pasturelands.

They climbed to the ridge, looked back down the Garth and tried to pick out their own cottage, but it was hidden behind a line of trees. Maybe it was better that way, she thought; they had come up here to get away from that vile slurry tide and its smell of putrefaction. In the far distance they could hear the steady *thump-thump-thump* of the rig and the roar of the compressor.

Mike took her hand and led her over on to the other side of the hill, where the only sounds were the drone of insects and the bleating of sheep. When they returned that evening the workmen would have gone, and only the stench would remain. She could taste it like bile in her throat even up here.

'Didn't Bennion mention something about them clearing up all their mess afterwards?' She asked.

'He *mentioned* it,' Mike replied, 'in passing. But I can't see how they can clear up all that sludge. Maybe they'll hose it away. But let's not spoil the afternoon thinking about it.'

They returned to Garth Cottage shortly before nine o'clock in the welcome cool of a heatwave's evening, having called in at the Bear, Garth's only pub, for a bar snack. Now they approached the cottage in trepidation.

The rotting odour met them at the gate as they squeezed past the silent compressor truck, an invisible cloud of malevolence which hovered over their home, waiting for them to come back. If anything, the smell was worse in the stillness of evening, more dominant without the accompanying deafening sounds of rig and compressor. Tangible – at least it touched them. Heavy in the windless atmosphere, not so much as a faint breeze to disperse it.

'Ugh!' Holly quickened her step, fumbling for her doorkey, desperate to be indoors when they should have been sitting on the patio enjoying the best hours of the day, watching the sun sink out of sight behind the Bryn. 'My God, it's worse than ever. We'll have to stifle ourselves with the windows closed tonight, Mike.'

'I wonder if they've finished drilling.' He looked back at the silent rig and slammed the door shut. 'I should think — '

The telephone rang in the kitchen, a jarring jangle as though it had been awaiting them with some message and now it could speak. They looked at each other in a moment of illogical fear, each willing the other to answer it.

'Garth 179.' Mike lifted the handset, aware that his voice was trembling slightly.

'Ah, Mr Mannion!' It was Bennion – there was no mistaking his confident businesslike voice. 'I've been trying to get you all evening.'

A veiled reprimand for being absent, Mike decided, and felt angry. We've been out because of your filthy smell, Bennion, he felt like saying. 'What can I do for you, Mr Bennion?' he asked.

'Bad news, I'm afraid, Mr Mannion.' The voice was loaded with false jocularity. *Sweeten the pill, soften the blow*.

'Oh?' Holly was at his side trying to listen.

'Our boys drilled down to sixty feet but there wasn't enough water. They had to go on until they found some.'

'How deep?' That advance on the landscape paintings was already diminishing.

'A hundred and thirty, I'm afraid!'

'Christ!' Rapid mental arithmetic told him 130 £7.50's less the original £850 made . . . £525!

'They stopped at sixty feet, as agreed, knocked the door to warn you that they'd have to go deeper, but you were out.'

'What's done is done.' Mike was suddenly philosophical.

'I just thought I ought to tell you.' Bennion sounded relieved that his news had not invoked an angry outburst.

'Thank you.' Mike avoided Holly's penetrating stare. 'Oh, just one thing, Mr Bennion. What's this awful smell that's coming up out of the well?'

'Smell, Mr Mannion? What smell? The lads never said anything about it when they came back in this evening.'

'It's like. . . .' Oh, Christ, what *was* it like? 'It's like . . .

something rotting, only a thousand times worse. You can taste it, it permeates everything.'

'Oh, I shouldn't worry about it,' Bennion laughed. 'It's probably just surface pollution, some kind of animal matter. We find it all over the place, but the shaft will be sealed so you've nothing to worry about. The lads have finished drilling. Tomorrow they'll put the submersible pump in, cement the pit in and seal it off. Take it from me, Mr Mannion, by Tuesday, Wednesday, maybe, you'll have the purest water in the district coming out of your taps. Don't worry about a thing.'

'And what about all this awful slurry that's burying the garden? You did mention that you'd clear up the mess after you'd finished.'

'We haven't finished yet!' Bennion's tone changed and became sharp with controlled irritation. 'When we've finished the job, all that will be hosed away.'

The line went dead, the conversation was closed. Slowly Mike Mannion replaced the receiver. He said to Holly, 'There's nothing whatever to worry about, just a bad smell that will disappear when they wash the slurry away.' He tried to sound relieved, confident. But only for his wife's sake, because his stomach was balling again and for some inexplicable reason he felt frightened.

Very frightened.

4

Nick Paton had moved out from the Midlands' sprawling conurbation shortly after passing his City & Guilds. A qualified plumber, he sought a change of lifestyle like many others who had opted out, and preferred to earn his living maintaining private water supplies run by hydraulic rams rather than conventional mains bursts, and overhauling central-heating systems operated by wood-burners in contrast to boring gas and electric ones. It promised a more relaxed way of life. But he had been disillusioned this last five years; because he was good he was in demand, and there came a time when the workload exceeded the number of hours available in the week. So he worked weekends to try to catch up. But he never caught up, he was fighting against a backlog of jobs, and the pleading phone calls became abusive. So he learned to live with it, left his telephone off the hook and took each day as it came.

Nick had seen his thirtieth birthday last February. He was tall and thin, and his hair was sparse; by the time he was forty his crown would be bald. But that was a long way off – he lived for today. His easy-going disposition was rarely ruffled; girls fancied him, older women, too, but he seemed oblivious to their attentions. There was barely time enough for work, certainly none for romance.

Three years ago he had moved out of his lodgings with Mrs Carter – an ageing widow who looked upon him as the son she had lost in the war – and bought the Green, a ramshackle cottage on the edge of Garth village. He somehow found the time to renovate it but was seldom at home to enjoy the results. It was a roosting place, somewhere to sleep, and he ate either at the Bear, if he was lucky enough to be finished work before the landlord called 'time', or else at a fish and chip shop in the town, seven miles away.

His list of proposed calls was scribbled on a jotter pad kept in his Escort van. The first job scheduled for that morning was Mrs King's toilet, the downstairs one. She had phoned the previous week, or it could have been a fortnight ago, to report that it 'bubbled back' when she flushed it. A blockage, undoubtedly, but he guessed it was nothing that a good rodding wouldn't solve. Ten minutes at the most, and then there would be some 'bait' for him, the Garth term for elevenses, a mug of tea and a pile of cheese and pickle sandwiches. No rush there, and he needn't bother with much breakfast this morning.

The the telephone bleeped. Damn, he had forgotten to take it off the hook. He decided to answer it, and that was a decision of mixed benefits. It was Frank Bennion on the line, and that meant he wouldn't be going to Mrs King's for bait.

In a way Bennion was his boss. The borehole man put a lot of work Nick's way; there were innumerable wells to pipe into dwellings and Bennion paid well – charged the customer plenty, too. Nick sighed beneath his breath. 'Very well, Mr Bennion, I'll go straight there this morning.'

There was one snag. This fellow at Garth Cottage – Nick knew the place vaguely and had thought it was still unoccupied – had water from a ram as well, and wanted the new system plumbed into the existing one. No real problem, just time-consuming; an extra pit, two stop-cocks, some modifications to the header tank in the loft. An extra day's work. He hoped Mrs King's toilet blockage had cleared itself. They often did. Nick lingered another ten minutes, just time enough to eat some beans on toast; there was unlikely to be bait at Garth Cottage.

The compressor was blocking the gateway so he had to park on the grass verge. From here he had a view of the drive, and saw that Tommy Eaton and Jim Fitzpatrick had already started digging the trench from the borehole to the house; it looked as if the water pipes entered beneath the front door, which meant that he would have very little trenching to do himself for the other system, maybe only a couple of yards or so. First, though, he needed to go up into the loft and look at the tank – that would be the tricky part. He glanced across the road. There was a council land drain going under it. What was the betting that old Hughes had used that to cross the road with his water pipe? Nick laughed to himself; out in the country, folk were predictable. He had learned that in a very short time.

Christ, there was a bloody stink! He coughed, looked towards the borehole and saw that slurry still dripped from the trees and was drying in the garden. That smell was never normal, he thought, more like something decomposing. He wished he had remembered to leave the phone off, and then he would have been at Mrs King's doing an easy routine job and eating cheese and pickle sandwiches when it was done. He shrugged his shoulders and trudged down the drive towards the cottage.

Holly Mannion opened the door to his knock. 'You must be the plumber.' She seemed embarrassed, and looked across to where the two workmen were still digging out the trench. That terrible smell was still hanging around although it did not seem quite so bad as yesterday. Perhaps it would disperse now that the sea of sludge was almost dry. 'Come in, please.'

'Thanks.' Nick squeezed inside and laid his tool bag on the floor. 'I'll have to have a look at the tank in the attic first to see what's to be done.'

'Tea or coffee?' She moved over to the stove where the kettle was boiling.

'Er . . . coffee, please.' His thoughts switched momentarily to Mrs King's, but there were unlikely to be sandwiches on offer here. His eyes rested on Holly; she was very attractive. Usually he was too wrapped up in his work to notice the opposite sex. He wondered idly where her husband was. Out at work, probably.

'I didn't realize that having a borehole meant such an upheaval.' She brought two steaming mugs of coffee to the table and seated herself opposite him. 'Or such an awful smell, for that matter.'

'Not very nice, is it?' He tried to make a joke of it but it didn't sound funny. 'Like a . . . well, a bit of a niff, to say the least.'

'What do you think has caused it?'

He scratched his head and tried to sound casual. After all, it was Bennion's pigeon, not his. 'I'd say they've drilled through an old boghole. But that won't matter,' he hastily tried to reassure her, 'because they'll seal the well at least twenty feet down. Blimey, some of the holes that Bennion's drilled have been in farmyards knee deep in sh – cowmuck.'

'I hope you're right. . .?'

'Nick.' He suddenly felt at ease with her. 'Well, I'd best get started. From what I've seen out there, Jim and Tommy are nearly finished. They'll be away this afternoon, I reckon.'

'Thank God for that,' She resisted the temptation to go and look out of the window. 'I shan't be sorry to see the back of them. Nothing personal, but it has been a disturbance. My husband's an artist, you see.'

'Oh!' Nick failed to keep the disappointment out of his tone. Subconsciously he was hoping that this girl was either separated or divorced, or maybe her husband worked away in the week. Not that it would have made any difference, she was hardly likely to fall in love with a plumber at first sight. 'I'll get on up to the attic, then.'

'I'll show you where the loft ladder is.' She walked through to the hall ahead of him, and he found himself fascinated by the rear view of her, in those ragged cut-off denim shorts. Suddenly he was glad he had answered the phone that morning and hadn't gone straight to fix Mrs King's toilet.

The men outside were loading up their equipment. Empty drums were stacked in the back of the Land Rover and the trailer was hitched on, filled with surplus rubble which they were taking away. They were hurrying even though it was already four-thirty. There was another job to set up ready for drilling in the morning; Frank Bennion did not delay where work was concerned. They heard an approaching car slow in the lane outside and park behind the plumber's van. That would be the boss – he seemed to sense completion time on every job by some kind of mysterious sixth sense, like his dowsing with the pendulum.

'Well, it looks as if they've finished.' There was distinct relief in Mike Mannion's voice as he watched from the kitchen window, a mug of tea in his hand. 'Here's Bennion, come to see that everything's satisfactory. Well, I don't think we've much to complain about – they've cleared up pretty well, even hosed all that sludge away. Most of it will trickle down old Hughes's field.' He gave a short laugh. 'But the borehole top looks pretty untidy. I thought they'd remove that length of blue pipe from it when they'd done. Anyway, here's Bennion coming now.'

'Everything to your satisfaction?' The boss was smiling benignly. 'Good lads, those. They always do a good job. Now, you'll note that we've left you that thirty foot of pipe on the well. That's for pumping the waste down the field. Pump it for two or three days to clean it out, then if you turn the stopcock next to it, and check that the switch in the box on the outside wall is turned on, you'll have water coming out of your taps. Oh, and make sure that the float switch is submerged in the tank in the loft. At the moment it's pulled out so that you can pump the water away.' He reached in his pocket and pulled out a neatly folded sheet of paper. 'And here's the damage, Mr Mannion.'

'Thank you.' Mike took it but did not open it out. 'As soon as the tests prove the water's pure I'll send you a cheque.'

'I don't think you need to worry about the quality of the water, Mr Mannion.' There was a sharp edge to Bennion's voice now. 'I've seen it coming out of the pipe. It's as clear as a bell.'

'I hope so.' Mike was wondering how long it would be before his contract signature money came through. He had returned the signed documents by this morning's post. 'Anyway, we'll see. I've already phoned the Environmental Health Department. Their inspector is calling to test the water the day after tomorrow. As I said, as soon as they give me the okay, I'll post you a cheque.'

'We usually receive payment on completion.' Bennion's smile had vanished. 'Naturally, if there are any teething problems we will rectify them at once. But when there are any, they are usually of a minor nature.'

'I'll pay you the moment we get the all-clear.' Mike dropped the invoice on to the table. 'As you said, Mr Bennion, no water, no fee. And we don't know yet whether it will be drinkable, do we?'

'Well, don't be too long about it.' Frank Bennion turned towards the door and jammed his soft hat angrily on his head – 'Good day to you both.'

They stood in the window, watching him stride back down the drive until he was lost from their view. Engines started up: the BMW, followed by the Land Rover, then the compressor truck.

'Well, that's that.' Holly sank down in the nearest chair. 'The plumber's fixing the original system into the new one, and then our problems are over. I hope. By the way, that stench seems to have gone. Whatever it was, they've obviously managed to clear it, Mike.'

'Thank God! Now all we need is the health inspector to test the water.' And my money through so that I can pay Bennion, he added silently, because he's not the type to be stalled for long.

Mike had an uneasy feeling, one that he could not place. Not just about the water but about this whole setup. He shrugged it off. There was no point in discussing illogical fears with Holly, but somehow the job was all too sudden to be passed off and forgotten; one week they were dry, the next they had all the water they needed. And that stench worried him; it was gone now, but he could still smell its lingering vile odour in his nostrils.

There were footsteps on the stairs, and they turned to see Nick Paton entering the room. He nodded to Mike, then dropped his gaze.

'How's it going, Nick?' Holly broke the sudden awkward silence.

'Okay.' He smiled faintly. 'I've finished upstairs. Now all I need to do is dig a pit outside the door and join the two pipes up in there. By this time tomorrow you'll be able to use whichever system you want. At least, you'll be able to use the ram again when it rains.' He laughed nervously. 'I'll see you first thing in the morning.'

Mike went back to his studio. Now that the drilling was finished he should have been able to concentrate on his painting. But for some reason he could not settle. This whole business had been most disturbing. And for some inexplicable reason it still was.

5

Mike had envisaged a young, possibly officious health inspector, modern bureaucracy in an office suit and green wellies, silently rebuking them for having opted out of a conventional life, offhand because they were wasting the department's time when they should have been living in suburbia and drinking mains water and gratefully accepting unquestioningly any additives which the authority in their infinite wisdom chose to put in it. But Bill Kemp was nothing like that at all, in fact he was the complete opposite of what Mike had imagined.

The man from the Environmental Health Department was, quite obviously, of retirement age – maybe a year or two over it. Tall, slightly stooped, he had a shock of white hair which flopped over his narrow forehead. His piercing grey eyes were shrewd but kindly behind rimless glasses. He wore a white cotton jacket and grey flannels which would have been more at home on the bowling green. The only hint of officialdom was the clipboard full of duplicated sheets and the small gas bunsen burner which he held in his other hand.

'It doesn't smell very good from here, does it?' He stood by the door, looking towards the unsightly mound of concrete and blue piping. 'Decidedly niffy, in fact.'

'It didn't smell good when they were drilling.' Mike's hopes sank. 'But the smell seemed to go once they'd finished.'

'Or maybe you'd got acclimatized to it.' The official was walking towards the borehole. Beyond the overgrown shrubbery which was the boundary between Garth Cottage and Elwyn Hughes's farm they could hear the gushing of water as the well continued to pump to waste. 'Now, I need to take two samples.' He produced a couple of corked empty test tubes. 'One from the borehole itself and the other from the taps.'

They walked into the field. Trespassing. Mike enjoyed the thought but was glad Hughes wasn't around. Right now he considered they had enough problems without the old farmer's intervention. The length of pipe lay in the browned grass, a half-coiled viper spitting its venom. Mike peered over Kemp's shoulder as the inspector dropped to his knees and managed to light the burner.

'Go and switch it off for a moment, will you, Mr Mannion?' he asked. 'I'll have to sterilize the end of the pipe first. A fly or a bit of dirt on there could result in a contaminated test. Then switch the water to the taps and I'll join you in the kitchen.'

Mike knelt by the open pit at the top of the borehole and saw the pipe jutting up out of its surrounds. It went down a hundred and thirty feet, unless Bennion was conning him, far into the earth. Darkness and cold, a deep evil, place. He grasped the red knob of the stopcock and even as he struggled to turn it in an anticlockwise direction, the stench hit him like a physical blow from some foul invisible demon and sent him reeling back, gasping for air. *Oh, Jesus Christ, the smell is still here!*

'Mike, are you all right?'

He looked up and saw Holly running towards him, an anguished expression on her face. He wanted to shout to her to keep away, to stay clear, but the words would not come. It was as though whatever it was that was down there was asphyxiating him. She was close now, did not seem to notice.

And then the foul air was gone, leaving only a rancid taste in his throat. 'I'm all right.' He tried to speak normally, but kept his head turned away from her. 'I've got to turn this stopcock. I . . . lost my balance.'

She did not reply; perhaps she believed him. With shaking fingers he grasped the knob again, and this time it turned easily.

'That's fine.' Kemp's voice came from the field beyond. A few seconds and then, 'Now go and put the floatswitch back in the tank.'

Holly followed him, right up the ladder into the dry, dusty loft, holding the torch, once flashing it on his face as though checking him again. Mike pulled up the switch on its length of cord and dropped it back into the half-filled tank. A faint splash, then a droplet of icy water flecked on his face and he recoiled in the blackness. *God, that water's come from down there, too!*

Now the water was flowing in, starting to fill up the tank. 'Let's go back downstairs.' Christ, he thought, I've got to come back up here, put my hand in *that* to pull the switch out again!

The health inspector was standing at the sink, the flame of his Bunsen burner playing on the cold tap. After a few seconds of intense heat he extinguished the flame, turned on the water and filled the second test tube. Meticulously he corked it and wrote something on the label.

'I'll have that into the laboratory by three o'clock this afternoon,' he smiled. 'Officially the test will take about a week, but I'll know the result in a day or two and I'll phone and let you know. These bacteriological tests are free, but if you want a chemical test it'll cost you fifty quid.'

'I think we'll stick with the bacteriological tests for the moment,' Mike replied. 'Have you . . . any ideas? I mean, can you tell anything at this stage?'

Kemp hesitated. 'Strictly, I'm not supposed to give an opinion. But all I can say is that the water itself looks clear enough but . . . well, when it was coming out of the pipe in the field there was a sort of . . . putrid smell, like the one I smelled when I arrived. Can't smell it now. It may be nothing, perhaps some of that slurry that's lying all over the field. Anyway, the lab tests will prove whether or not the water's fit to drink. As I said, I'll phone you.'

'All we can do is keep our fingers crossed.' Mike stood on the patio with Holly after Kemp had gone. 'If it wasn't for that stink, I'd say by the look of it the water's pure.'

Nick Paton had finished and left, and for the first time for days Garth Cottage seemed strangely deserted. Mike had almost finished his second landscape. It was much easier to work now. That feeling of mounting tension had gone, along with the vile odour, and the only inconvenience was having to fetch several containers of water for domestic use from the outside tap on the garage forecourt in the village.

'It's a farcical situation.' He lifted a polythene water carrier up on to the working surface next to the sink. 'Here we are with, in theory, *two* water supplies, and we're having to fetch the bloody stuff daily from the village! Still, hopefully it won't be for long. With luck, Kemp will phone tomorrow.'

'And inform us of the worst,' Holly replied.

'Don't be a bloody pessimist.'

'Well, I know it won't be fit to drink.' Holly's depression had been deepening all day. She had woken with it and, like a headache, it had got worse and worse. 'The inspector knew, but he didn't say because he wasn't allowed to, just hinted.'

'Well, you dragged me out here away from the town comforts,' he retorted. 'And only last week you said that life here was idyllic and you could stand it for the rest of your life. Don't tell me you've changed your mind, Holly.'

'I was fine until they started drilling.' She was very close to tears now. 'Then everything seemed to change, and this place became . . . *evil*.'

He wanted to tell her it was nonsense, but he knew he would be lying if he did. The stench that came up out of the bowels of the earth was both tangible and malevolent. Like Satan's foul breath from hell!

'Well, it's gone now, whatever it was.' He slipped an arm around her. 'And if you want to sell up, then just say so.'

'I don't.' She was adamant. 'Not yet, anyway. Let's wait and see what the tests throw up.'

Outside, the sun blazed fiercely, scorching up the surrounding countryside. A place of peace and tranquillity; it was difficult now to imagine it as anything else.

It was Friday morning, and there was still no word from Bill Kemp. Mike was edgy; he sensed Holly's restlessness, too. He was tempted to phone the Environmental Health Department but he resisted the urge. In all probability Kemp would not be there; his was only a part-time retirement job checking private water supplies. Or the laboratory had not sent the tests through yet; like that time when Holly had toxoplasmosis and it had taken three lots of tests to diagnose the problem. Patients became frustrated, but bureaucracy went along at its usual pedestrian pace, devoid of emotion. The health officials didn't care. All they had to do was to test a sample of water, and they would do it in *their* time.

He had finished the second landscape. It looked fine, but he sensed a lack of feeling in it, though perhaps that was only obvious to him. He hoped so, anyway. A workmanlike job by a professional artist, he judged, no way a masterpiece with feeling. It left a sense of dissatisfaction, a longing to be back in a terraced house with no outside problems, just his work to concentrate on. Maybe it would be a blessing in disguise if the tests were positive, a valid reason for selling up. At heart he was a townie, and he would never be otherwise.

And then the phone rang. Mike knew even before he went through to the kitchen that it was Kemp on the line. Holly had answered it, she was holding the receiver out to him, almost shying away from it.

'Kemp here.' The health inspector's tone said all that Mike feared, a kind of 'it's bad news, I'm afraid' voice. 'I've just had the results of your water test in this morning. I'm afraid the well's contaminated!'

'I see.' He was trying to keep it from Holly, which he knew was stupid because she was standing right by him and would find out from the rest of the conversation. 'How bad?'

'*Very bad*!' Kemp paused. Mike could hear a rustling of paper. 'A variety of bacilli, salmonella included – twenty-five per cent. Others which will need a chemical test if you want them isolated. But that will cost you fifty quid. I'm sorry.'

Mike stiffened. Salmonella itself was bad enough – sheep droppings washed down from Hughes' pasture-land probably. The rest unknown poisons. Bureaucracy didn't care, they'd done all that was asked of them. '*Disease?*'

'I couldn't say, I'm not a scientist, but they probably wouldn't do you any good if you took them into your system.'

'What do you suggest?'

'You could pump the well to waste for another few days, see if you can clear it. Apart from that, I can't suggest anything.'

Oh, shit! We've been pumping the well for days, and if it was going to clear it would have done so by now, he thought. *And suddenly he could taste that foulness in his mouth again, a cloying putrefaction like residue on his palate from some vile cesspit.*

'I'll get back to Bennion.' His voice sounded as if it was a whisper coming from a distance. 'Maybe he'll know what to do.' And if he doesn't, I'm two and a half grand better off and we can move to some civilized place, he consoled himself. Now he had to console Holly.

'You do that, Mr Mannion. And when you want another test, just give me a bell. All the best.'

'So it *is* bad.' Holly covered her face with her hands. 'I knew it couldn't be otherwise after I'd smelled it. Oh, Mike, *it's more than just contaminated, it's evil!*'

'That's nonsense.' Mike knew he would fail to convince his wife, but he had to say something. The responsibility was his, but right now he was going to pass the buck . . . to Frank Bennion. Holding the receiver, he dialled with a finger of the same hand, his other arm cradling Holly to him. He heard the phone ringing at the other end.

A woman's voice answered, probably Bennion's wife. Bennion was around somewhere, she said, and she'd go and fetch him. An agonizing two minutes passed before he heard Frank Bennion's suave voice.

'Ah, Mr Mannion, you've phoned to tell me that — '

'That the well's contaminated. Badly. Salmonella and a host of other so far unidentified bugs. The bloody thing's a foul boghole.'

Bennion caught his breath, but when he spoke again the confidence was back in his voice. 'Not to worry, Mr Mannion. Just a teething problem. I'll tell you what the problem is, one of the seals on the liner is probably faulty and is letting in surface contamination. We can rectify it easily enough.'

'How?' Mike was abrupt. I'd sooner not have to pay you and get the hell out of here, he thought.

'I'll have the lads there first thing in the morning. They can winch the liner out, check the seals and put it right. Just bear with me for a couple of days or so. Not to worry, when we've finished you'll have pure water, I guarantee it.'

'All right,' he said grudgingly, wishing they could call the deal off, fill the hell-hole in and bury that evil forever. But Frank Bennion wanted his money, and he wouldn't give up without a fight. 'See you tomorrow, then.'

'It won't be any good.' Holly groaned. 'It's hopeless. There's *something* down there, I know it.'

'Salmonella and friends.' Mike unscrewed a water-container, filled the kettle and put it on the stove to boil.

'More than that. Much more. Oh, Mike, I'm so frightened.'

He did not reply. Because he was frightened too, against all logic, all reasoning. Because he knew that the stench which had come up at him out of the well the other day had been a *living* force, an evil entity.

And whatever it was, it was still down there. Waiting. For what?

6

Holly felt a sense of despair as she watched the Land Rover backing the rig down through the gateway again. The compressor truck was parked in the entrance. It was like a rerun of some terribly boring film that she had seen only yesterday, and she hated the idea of having to sit through it again. Tommy Eaton and Jim Fitzpatrick were busily fixing up the winch on the back of the vehicle to the protruding blue pipe which was the top of the well liner, tying ropes, making sure that they were firm enough, then pausing to light cigarettes.

Holly glanced at the clock above the Rayburn. Nine-five. They had not wasted any time getting here; Bennion was obviously a man of his word. Or, more likely, and she smiled wryly to herself, money was his god. There was a bill outstanding because of a hitch, so the priority was to rectify it and get his money. She wondered how Mike was going to pay. The signature money would not be arriving just yet – it might be another week or two. Still, water tests took time; Kemp would have to be summoned, do his testing and submit it to the laboratory, and they certainly wouldn't hurry. It all took time and, right now, time was of the essence.

A sudden thought brought a sense of light relief: they wouldn't have to drill again, would they? Her reasoning told her that they had reached water, fresh or pure, and there was no point in going down any deeper. Just a question of hauling the liner out, checking the seals and dropping it back down the shaft. She shrugged. She hadn't a clue about the technicalities of water-well making, so it was a waste of time surmising. But she fervently hoped that that awful vibration, the noise and the spouting liquid filth jetting on to the trees and shrubs, dripping down and oozing all over the untended garden, would not happen again.

Footsteps on the stairs, and seconds later Mike appeared in the kitchen doorway dressed in a T-shirt and jeans. He had risen late. He was never an early riser, but this morning Holly noticed he looked tired and dispirited. All this business was getting him down, too. He poured himself a mug of coffee and sipped it before he spoke.

'I'll have to get cracking on that painting today,' he grunted, 'borehole or no borehole.'

'Which doesn't sound as though you relish the job,' she replied. 'I always thought artists were devoted to their work and loved every second of it. Where's your inspiration going to come from in that kind of mood?'

'Inspiration is a myth.' He added some more milk to his coffee. 'This is work, pure and simple, a commercial enterprise done for money. Hack work, if you like to put it into perspective.'

'I see.' She glanced out of the window as a clanking,

grinding noise began. 'That looks like the liner on its way up. Well, let's just hope they don't start drilling again.'

'There must be a possibility, otherwise they wouldn't have brought the rig, would they?'

'Gee, thanks.' Mike could be a bit touchy first thing in a morning. She had learnt that during the three years they had been married. 'Well, I'm going into town this morning. There's lots of things we're running low on. Coffee, for one thing.'

'You won't get the car out.' He nodded his head to where the big truck was blocking the entrance.

She almost said, 'You should have put it up on the road last night when you knew they were coming back,' but thought better of it. 'The bus runs today, ten-fifteen from the Green, back at three o'clock, so I'll see you after three. Have a good day.'

He grunted again. It wasn't going to be a good day. He didn't want it to be, because he was pissed off with all this business which wouldn't solve their water problem at the finish, he was sure of that. Frustration and inconvenience, that was all it amounted to. Thank Christ he had stuck to his guns and refused to pay. Eventually Bennion would have to admit defeat and fill his bloody hole in, and that would be that. Everything for nothing.

'That bleedin' stink's back again,' Tommy Eaton said through a mouthful of cold bacon sandwich as he struggled to push the sliding side window of the Land Rover shut. 'Jeez, I never smelled owt like it, Jim.'

'Huh?' His stocky, morose companion grunted as he avidly continued reading the sports page of his crumpled newspaper. 'The Town are trying to get that defender from Bristol on a free transfer for the start of the season. Another buckshee throw-out that nobody else wants. If you ask me. . . .'

'I said that fucking smell has started up again.' There were flies crawling over the insides of the windows, and was it any wonder! 'Your bloody nose must be stopped up, Jim!'

'Uh?'

'It *smells* out there. Which is why I've shut the window.'

'You don't expect anything else, do you? In this job you're working in shit all the time, drilling down through soak 'oles and . . . do you remember that time we tapped a septic-tank drain at the farm?'

'But nothin's ever smelled as bad as *this*!' Tommy could even taste it now, as if the bacon in his sandwich had gone off; putrid, worse than a sewage works. 'I tell you, Jim, it's giving me a bloody headache and a sore throat.'

'You'll get acclimatized to it shortly.' Jim Fitzpatrick had moved on to the racing page; if there had been a bookmaker's handy, he would have put a bet on Scarlet Lady in the three-thirty at Ludlow. But there wasn't a bookie in Garth, so he would just have a bet with himself and an extra pint tonight if it came up. 'We got used to it before, didn't we?'

'We should've sealed right down to twenty feet in the first place.' Tommy was obliquely blaming his companion for the oversight which had brought them back here. 'Then we wouldn't've had to get the bleedin' thing back up again.'

'Why worry? We're getting paid whether we're drilling new ones or repairing old ones. The only one to lose out is that old fart, Bennion.'

'Well, I don't like this bugger.' Tommy wrapped the remains of his sandwich in its greaseproof paper, put it back in his Tupperware box and made sure the lid fitted snugly. He didn't feel like eating. His usual ravenous appetite was non-existent this morning. Ugh, he could taste that stink as if it really was the bacon gone off. 'The sooner we're done and gone, the better. And make sure the fucker's sealed properly this time, Jim!'

'You leave that to *me*.' Fitzpatrick scowled beneath his grimy complexion. 'I'll say what's to be done on these jobs, lad. You're just the bloody mate. Get it?'

'I guess so,' the younger man sighed. The last thing he wanted was an argument. Jim was touchy this morning – he'd been on the beer last night, all right. 'I want to finish early tonight.'

'You'll be lucky, mate. This is a two-day job, as much work as starting from scratch, and the boss won't wear any 'angin' about 'cause time's money. There could be a bit of overtime in it if we play our cards right, so don't go fuckin' it up for me – 'cause I've got a wife and three kids to support. Goin' shaggin' that bird of yours again, I suppose?'

Tommy blushed slightly. It felt like a hot flush, the sort you got when you had a fever coming on. He always felt embarrassed when Jim started on these sexual innuendoes; the fellow didn't let up. Today, particularly, he could not be bothered to think of an apt reply. Ignore it, he told himself. Go on, finish reading your bloody paper, then we'll get back to work. Tommy felt lethargic. He could have closed his eyes and dozed off. Sometimes Jim had a snooze at bait-time; Christ, I wish you'd go to bloody sleep right now, he thought.

' 'Ad it last night, did you?' A coarse leer. 'Bloody knackered you by the look of it. I wouldn't've thought that wench of yours 'ad it in 'er to knacker you. All right on the job, is 'er?'

Tommy closed his eyes and did not reply. His head was pounding, he felt slightly sick and that awful stench was in his nose and throat. He was sure it wasn't healthy, and couldn't possibly do him any good. What was that disease they used to get years ago from drains and the like? He remembered how his mother went on about it when he was very young. Diphtheria, that was it. Kids died from it until they found a vaccine. So it couldn't be diphtheria because it didn't exist any more. Something else, then. There was always a new virus, one that baffled the doctors. They didn't find a cure until somebody had died. He was trembling. He was going to be ill, he knew that. Really ill, a high temperature, sweating, aching all over. Jim was saying something but Tommy was not listening, aware he might have to go home shortly.

'Come on.' Jim was shaking his younger companion roughly. 'Time to start work. We can't sit in 'ere all day, stink or no stink.'

Tommy Eaton groaned and forced himself up out of the seat. Those flies on the windscreen seemed to spin, crazy black dots that were joining up into a gyrating circle. Outside there was a fog, a heat haze, perhaps, rolling in at him. He clutched the steering wheel, holding on grimly.

'What's up, Tommy?' Jim was genuinely concerned now.

'I . . . I'll be all right.' The buzzing flies were coming apart now, separating, and outside the fog was rolling back, clearing until it was all gone. He was sweating – but that was the heat, the stifling atmosphere of the closed Land Rover he told himself. His headache had receded a little. He'd be all right – he'd have to be, because there was no way he could go home. No transport, except the Land Rover and the big truck, and Bennion would not stand for either being used for private reasons. And as he had to stay, there was no point in doing anything other than work. His legs felt shaky and all the strength seemed to have drained from his body. He knelt down and began unscrewing one of the seals on the liner; it was stiff, so he had to exert every vestige of force he could muster. And when it finally came apart he let out a loud gasp.

'I tell you, you're bleedin' knackered. Too much dick, that's your trouble.' Jim Fitzpatrick did not glance up. 'Tell you sommat else, son. That wench of your'n is after more than just a good shaggin', you mark my words. I got caught just the same as you will, and look at me, kids and 'avin' to work every minute Bennion'll let me, for *them*. She'll say to you one o' the nights, "there's no need to use one o' them french letters, Tommy, 'cause I'm safe for a day or two." So you'll put it in, come your lot and think it's bleedin' great. Next thing you know, she'll be makin' a show o' bein' upset and sobbin' "Tommy, I'm in the club, we'll 'ave to get married." It's the same old story, and the blokes fall for it every time. I did, and you will, too. See if I'm not right, my son.'

Tommy's brain spun and he almost fell forward on to his face. Jim's words rang in his ears, echoed, took on a taunting tone. *Oh, Christ, why did you have to tell me that today, Jim?*

Last night . . . it was as though Jim Fitzpatrick had been looking through a peephole into the council house where Penny lived with her parents, and now was throwing it all back in his face. Penny's folks were away at Bridlington for the week, so she and Tommy had made the best of their chance. They couldn't get up to Penny's room fast enough each evening. Penny was no oil painting, he was the first to admit that, but her slim figure was reasonable, and what was it Jim had muttered the other week. . .? You don't look at the mantelpiece when you're poking the fire.

They had played about, enjoying their freedom. It was much more relaxed than a screw in the back of the old van or up in the wood where somebody might come along. She had played with him, got him really close, and when he leaned across to try and find that packet of condoms he'd left handy on top of his pile of clothes by the bed, she had pulled him back.

'You needn't worry about *that* tonight, Tommy, I'm safe for a day or two. Go on, shoot it all into me *please*!'

Tommy had done just that, and it had been the most marvellous sensation of his young life. In fact, he had done it twice, the second time about an hour later. It *had* worried him, there was no point in denying it hadn't, but he hoped it would be all right; he would probably worry for weeks.

Now grumpy old Jim had said the very words Tommy didn't want to hear. And there was a chilling ring of fear about them. Christ, he wouldn't want to *marry* Penny! That voice of hers, a kind of complaining screech most of the time coming out of a mouth that took on a square shape when she was building herself up for a tantrum. He could see it now, hear it, the wail, 'I'm pregnant, Tommy. We'll *'ave* to get married!'

Anger, dismay and a sensation of nausea brought back the pounding in his temples and made him sweat rivulets. Then he was shivering in the heat.

'Blimey, you ain't gone and done it already, 'ave you, son?'

He did not reply. The mist was back before his eyes, an opaqueness tinted with crimson. His throat was dry, and that smell was clogging his nostrils – the stench of rotting, diseased flesh!

Jim did not appear to notice. He was busy unpacking some new seals, whistling tunelessly through his breath. And that was when Tommy Eaton looked down at his own body and stared in horrified disbelief.

At first he thought it was some kind of skin rash spreading downwards from his navel and disappearing from view into his worn jeans. A mass of tiny pimples, dozens of them, were standing out starkly red against the sun-tanned skin. He resisted the urge to undo his belt, drop his trousers and see where this sudden disfigurement ended. In a minute he'd go into the bushes and do just that. For the moment, he was too shocked at what he saw. Pull yourself together, he told himself. It's probably a nettle rash, or some other foliage that you're allergic to. The pimples stung, and he was suddenly aware of a kind of burning sensation. When he rubbed them, they stung even more sharply and seemed to swell. He covered them with his hands in case Jim noticed them. It wasn't the clap, was it? His companion was always making jokes about catching a dose of 'the clap'. It depended if the pimples spread right down *there*. Or came up from *there!*

'We'll 'ave to winch the pump up as well,' Jim was saying, his back to Tommy. 'Tell you somethin', we'll be lucky to be finished by tomorrow at this rate. Never mind, we're gettin' paid for it.'

God, he needed a drink, his throat was on fire, scalding him. Tommy glanced round. He needed water, fast. A whiff of the well had him recoiling. It was poisoned, for sure. The only place where there was any drinking water available was in those containers the Mannions filled up daily down at the garage in the village. He started for the house, his steps unsteady.

'Hey, where you goin', Tommy?'

'To get a drink.'

'Use yer flask in the truck, lad. We're busy, we ain't got time for goin' in search o' bloody water.'

Tommy did not reply. He ignored Jim. He was at the back door now, thumping feebly on the peeling paintwork, each knock vibrating through his entire body. *Oh, come on! Bloody well answer. I need water!*

His knocking grew weaker; he could hear them echoing in the kitchen. Where the fucking hell had that woman got to? He wanted to shout, to curse, to sob. *Can't you see I'm burning up. I'm dying! I've got something that looks like the fucking clap.'*

'Can I help you?' Mike Mannion appeared round the side of the house, an expression of annoyance on his bearded face at this sudden interruption. 'I'm very busy, you know.'

'Water . . . please!' It was like an old desert movie, Tommy thought, mouthing his plea, his mouth so parched that he could barely get the words out. His saliva had all gone and now there was a dull pain where that inexplicable rash was. He kept it covered with his hands, wondering if he looked like somebody starting appendicitis pains. He didn't care – anything so long as this bloke gave him water.

'You sure you're okay, laddie?'

'I'm fine. It's just . . . the heat.'

'And that bloody smell.' Mike pinched his nostrils. 'Phew, it's as if something had died and was rotting in the sun. Come on in, I'll find you a drink. We've got some cordial somewhere if I can find it.'

'Water, please. Just . . . *water.*'

'Here you are, then.' Colourless liquid glugged into a plastic beaker. 'You want to watch it out there with that stench. You might get cholera or something.'

Tommy grabbed the beaker, slopping some of the contents. He drank noisily, water running down his chin, dripping on to his chest and on to the quarry-tiled floor. Slurping, an animal at the waterhole, then he sucked on the empty container, head back, trying to drain the last dregs.

'Here, have some more. Blimey, you've got a thirst!'

'Thanks.' Tommy emptied the second fill-up and put the beaker on the table. 'I needed that. It's the heat.' He felt slightly better. Now there was just a smarting in his lower regions. Maybe that bloody girl had given him the clap. It wasn't beyond the bounds of possibility; she boasted how she'd been around before she met him, and about all the blokes who had had her. She *might* just be two-timing him, screwing with some dirty sod on the side. And there were worse things around these days than VD. . . . The thought struck Tommy for the first time and he almost fainted. He had to clutch at the edge of the table to save himself from falling.

'Look, matey, I think you're ill. I'll get the car out and take you home.' There was real concern in Mike Mannion's voice. A trace of fear, too. He had just caught sight of those sores on the youth's abdomen; they looked decidedly nasty. They were weeping thick revolting pus:

'No, I'm all right. Honest. Please.'

'All right. But I'm only in the studio round the other side of the house if you want me. And I'll leave the kitchen open in case you want another drink. Really, though, I thing you ought to go home and call a doctor.'

Alone in his bedroom, Tommy confirmed his worst fears. From his navel right down into his crotch, his flesh was just a rash of open sores that oozed matter like burst boils when he squeezed the pus out with finger and thumb.

Except that in this case he just went on squeezing; the stuff came out in never-ending syrupy streams, and, God, how it stank! Just like that foul odour that drifted up out of the Mannions' borehole. He heaved, dashed to the toilet and threw up what little he had eaten earlier in the day.

Standing there, he stared at the putrefying flesh in sheer terror and utter disbelief. *It was as though it was decomposing on his bones, a spreading gangrene!* Wheezing as he breathed, with the fever hot upon him, he felt dizzy and vomited again, but there was nothing left inside him to throw up.

Thank Jesus his mother was out, he thought. She had gone to bingo and left his supper in the oven. Food! The very thought had him retching bile, which burned his parched throat. He was panicking, crying. Then somehow he got himself under control.

He was going to die, he was certain of it. A terrifying thought, except that when your flesh is being eaten away before your eyes by a stinking spreading cancer you just want to get it over with. He stared at himself in the bedroom mirror with fevered eyes, scarcely recognizing himself.

The bitch, the fucking little whore, she had given him this! The poxy cow had passed on some awful disease. His anger turned to fury, erupting in hoarse, whispered curses; then simmering.

She would pay for this, he swore, oh, by Christ, she would! His sticky hands clenched, he shook his fists in the air. Whatever else, she would get what was coming to her. And, after all, he laughed – a cracked maniacal sound – they couldn't really do an awful lot to him. He'd be one big festering sore puking out whatever was left inside by the time they caught up with him!

Tommy dressed in a checked shirt and jeans, the feel of the material sore against his burning, festering body but at least it hid the still growing sores. The matter was soaking into his clothes and the stench was overpowering. He slunk out to his van and felt the warm stickiness in the seat of his trousers as he got behind the wheel, like bleeding piles. Driving slowly, erratically in places, twice he kerbed and heard pedestrians shout after him. A horn blared behind him; he ignored it. *Fuck 'em!* Finally he saw the council estate where Penny lived, took a wide sweep and almost collided with a boy on a bicycle. He saw the rider fall off and sprawl in the road. *Serve him bloody well right!*

His vision was distorted. He could not determine whether he had parked right up against the kerb or whether he was a yard from it. It did not matter. Trying to walk steadily, he seemed to be weighted down on the one side like a chronic back sufferer with a damaged spine. There was nobody about, or if there was he did not see them.

He opened the back door and stepped inside the small kitchen. There was a roaring in his ears and all he could smell was himself. Just standing there, squinting around him, he had to hold on to the old Belling cooker.

'Is that you, Tommy?' The distant shout sounded like a faint echo in underground caverns. *Who the fuck do you think it is, you poxy bitch?*

'Yes,' he tried to shout, but it came out in a strangled wheeze and made him cough and splatter scarlet droplets on the greasy floor. He was aware of the taste of blood.

'Come on up. I'm upstairs, my love.'

You whore! He pictured her lying there on the cramped single bed, her legs lewdly spread, laughing as she sought to arouse him. One last screw, my darling, he vowed, and I'll give *you* something you hadn't bargained on!

The curtains were closed in the bedroom. The sombre gloom was perhaps meant to hide the untidiness, the strewn clothing, her dirty bras, knickers and sweaty blouses which she was leaving for her mother to gather up and wash. A crumpled bed with the sheets thrown back, and Penny was lying in the middle as he had anticipated, naked and waiting, eyes closed as she played with herself in a crude attempt to arouse him. She laughed softly but did not look at him.

'I'm in the mood tonight, my darling,' she breathed, and he saw how her bosom was rising and falling.

So am I, he thought, and fumbled to undress, kicking away his jeans, popping a button on his shirt as he ripped it off. Naked, he clambered up on to the bed and knelt over her, waiting. *Feel me, sweetheart.*

Her hand came up, fingers stretched and flexing, and made contact with the shadowy silhouette which towered over her. A sharp intake of breath as her fingertips sank into something soft and spongy, warm and sticky, stroked a slime that gave off nauseating vile vapours. That was when Penny jerked up, saw him and started to scream.

'*Oh, my God! Tommy?*'

She wasn't even sure that it was him, and thought at first that it could not possibly be. No, it was surely a demented diseased stranger, some cancerous monstrosity bent on a final depravity before whatever was eating away his body claimed him for its own. Sheer terror almost snapped her mind, then cruelly left her her sanity so that she might suffer.

Her screams were stifled as he flung himself upon her, lowered his body down on to her distorted face and crushed her lips with that stinking morass. A squelch of bursting ulcers, the poison spraying in all directions, spotted the off-white walls with treacly grey and crimson.

He cried out in pain as the fire from his open groin travelled upwards, hastening to take him, and fought against it. His fingers squeezed in between their pressed bodies and slid through the spreading pus until they closed over her throat. Now he had the strength. He held down her kicking, flaying body and felt her gasping for breath underneath him, shuddering as she slowly suffocated.

Through his own agonized writhings he could feel her dying, her futile struggles growing weaker, and then at last she was just lying inert beneath him. He tried to laugh, but nothing came. He could not even see now. Nor hear. A blind, deaf creature sinking down on the corpse under him, he was waiting to join her in blissful death.

He was not even aware of the pounding footsteps on the stairs, the bedroom door crashing open and the screams of terror from those who had pursued him from the street below as they recoiled from the stench and horror of that barely living being which was slumped on the bed, its life oozing steadily from its festering body.

A crowd clustered on the tiny landing, ghouls who might have gathered gleefully at the scene of motorway carnage. But they had suddenly met their ultimate in depraved voyeurism, and their sick minds could not cope. Screaming, they clutched at one another, until finally the siren of an approaching police car quietened them.

7

Holly was upstairs in the bathroom. Mike was still working in his studio; he might be there for another couple of hours, he wasn't ruled by any timetable. In the beginning this had been difficult to come to terms with but they had reached an amicable arrangement: no set meal times. In the summer months Holly prepared a cold meal and they ate when Mike was ready; in the winter, a stew or something similar which could simmer without spoiling. Learning to live with an artist was not easy, but once she had adjusted to the ways of a creative person it became tolerable. He was touchy when a painting was tricky. Sometimes she did not see him for hours, and when she did the conversation was usually abrupt, sometimes non-existent. Other times he was euphoric.

He was unpredictable, but she accepted him as he was, would not have wished him to change.

God, that smell, it was worse than ever! She tipped some water out of a bucket into the basin and washed her hands. A sudden thought occurred to her, logical but disconcerting: perhaps the septic tank was full and needed emptying. Or the soakaway was blocked. This was another problem that they would have to face in the country. But if the stench *was* coming from the septic tank, then it made her feel a lot easier. Far rather a logical explanation than one connected with their water supply. She shuddered at the thought of the depth of that well. A hundred and thirty feet! Underground places gave her the creeps; it was best not to think about it.

Holly was tired. She had not enjoyed her trip into town, rather she had hated it – crowds, people jostling her on the pavements, queues at every checkout point in the supermarket. It had been a retrograde step, in a way. Here they were, living in a remote area, finally away from the hurly-burly of urban life, and she had gone right back into it. A few hours had seemed an eternity. If she had had the car then she would have come home as soon as she had finished her shopping. But time had dragged as she waited for the bus. She would have to go to town regularly, she accepted that. The village shop only catered for very basic needs; country folk weren't into things like decaffeinated coffee, pasta, wholegrain rice and natural foods. Anyway, she couldn't afford to shop at Stortons, however pleasant the elderly couple were.

The phone was ringing. She started, then made for the bathroom door. She had not seen Mike since her return, but she knew better than to go and disturb him with small talk when he was busy. At least, she presumed he was busy.

She was at the top of the stairs when the ringing stopped and she heard her husband's voice. She stood there, feeling a twinge of guilt because she was, in effect, eavesdropping. Don't be silly, she told herself, we both make and receive calls when the other's around. It's probably business, anyway.

It was. She heard Mike say, 'Hi, Bob, I half-guessed it might be you.' Holly knew it was Bob Daniels, Mike's agent, probably phoning to say he had the money in for the advance on the paintings. Or to say it had not arrived yet. She moved down a few steps, subconsciously letting her husband know she was there. She felt better about it that way, rather than listening in a sneaky fashion up on the landing.

'Oh, I see.' Mike sounded pleased, so it had to be good news. 'No. No problem at all. It's a bit inconvenient – I was hoping to finish the second landscape tomorrow – but it's not vital. I'll have to check the train times, I've not travelled to London from here yet. Ten-thirty sounds a bit tight. Maybe I could get a train tonight. Look, I'll phone the station and call you right back. Give me five minutes. Cheers.'

Mike looked up and saw Holly on the stairs. He was already thumbing through the bulky telephone directory. 'Won't be more than a few minutes. I have to go to London. Tonight, maybe.'

'Oh?' She felt a sinking in her stomach. She always did when Mike was going away.

'It was Bob, as you might have guessed. Another firm has come in for me. Book covers. There seems to be some urgency, one of their artists has let them down. They want to see me and my portfolio. I have to be there by ten-thirty tomorrow morning.' He was already dialling – Holly presumed it was British Rail. She moved on downstairs and put the kettle on the stove. The station might take some time to answer. Or the phone might have been deliberately left off the hook.

Much to her surprise, Mike was talking again. He'd got through. Times of trains to London? The clerk was looking them up. Then Mike said, 'I'll have to get the eight-thirty tonight then. Many thanks.'

Holly's stomach was busy knotting itself up. She

glanced at the clock: five-forty. They had plenty of time, but they still had to eat and she would have to pack a few things for him.

A sudden feeling of loneliness almost made her despair. When would he come back? Tomorrow night? It was unlikely. The day after, then? When they lived in the Midlands, London had been just a two-hour train journey – out of the house at eight, home by seven at the latest. Now it seemed so far away, another planet almost. She would be left here in Garth Cottage on her own. Suddenly that was a daunting prospect. Because of . . . the borehole? *How bloody stupid and childish can you get, Holly Mannion?*

'I should be back the day after tomorrow.' It was as if Mike had read her thoughts. He was piling salad on to a plate, cutting a slice of bread off the loaf. 'It's a bloody nuisance, having to go, but I can't afford not to. One day you're wondering where the work is coming from, the next it's piling in on you. Mustn't complain. Oh, by the way' – he was talking with his mouth full, something which annoyed her intensely at other times – 'that lad, Bennion's workman, he looked really ill this afternoon, as if he'd got a fever. I gave him some water, offered to take him home but he went back to work. Must have been okay, though, because they both left at five. They must be coming back tomorrow because they've gone home in the Land Rover and left the rest of the tack here. They seem to have put the liner back in the well. I hope to God everything's all right now. You'll be okay whilst I'm away, won't you?'

'Of course.' She hardly trusted herself to speak and her eyes were misty. 'I just wish they'd given you a bit more notice, though.'

'That's the way it goes in this business; they sit around on their backsides and then decide that they want something by tomorrow at the latest, if not sooner. You'd better run me into the station and bring the car back. I'll phone you sometime tomorrow and let you know when

I'm coming back so that you can pick me up. Must dash.' He pushed his empty plate away, scraped his chair back and made for the stairs. 'Pack me the essentials, will you, darling?'

Holly watched the train pull out of the station, waved until it was out of sight, then walked slowly back to the car. The loneliness crowded in on her. She almost thought about making the long drive to her mother's on the outskirts of Birmingham, then decided that was stupid, she and her mother would only argue for the evening and long into the night. About Mike. Her mother would never accept him, because he had left his first wife for Holly and might take a fancy to a third woman! Pull yourself together and get back to Garth Cottage, she told herself. You've enough work there to keep you busy for months, and it'll pass the time.

It was as she approached the cottage that she saw the police Metro parked on the verge behind the big yellow truck. Her stomach really knotted this time, her heart started to pound wildly. Something was wrong. Mike? No, she had only left him twenty minutes ago. Her mother? What?

'Mrs Mannion?' A plain-clothes detective got out of the car together with a uniformed constable. They smiled reassuringly. They always did that before they broke bad news to you, she thought. 'May we come inside and have a word with you?'

'Of course.' Her voice trembled, her legs seemed barely capable of supporting her weight as she led them to the door, and she almost dropped her key. In the uneasy silence, she had a feeling of fear, and guilt. Had she unknowingly broken the law in some way? She would soon find out.

'A young man was working here today, by the name of Tommy Eaton.' The detective stood by the window, forming a silhouette so that Holly was unable to see his features. 'Was he . . . did he seem all right to you?'

'I. . . .' She fought off a nervous stammer. 'I've been away most of the day . . . shopping. My husband said . . . I've just seen Mike off on the train to London . . . he said that the boy looked ill . . . as if he had a fever or something. He gave him some water. But Mike said he must be okay because they finished the day's work and went home. Is – is anything wrong, officer?'

'We shall need to speak to your husband, obviously. When will he be back from London?'

'I don't know.' Her words came in a rush. 'Tomorrow or the next day. What's happened?'

The detective glanced at the uniformed officer and there was a moment's heavy silence, a kind of 'I suppose we'll have to tell her eventually so we might as well now'. 'I'm afraid Tommy Eaton is dead!'

'*Dead!*'

'Yes.'

'But how?'

'That will be for the coroner to decide.' His tone was suddenly formal, official. 'An illness of some kind – we don't know at this stage, but it was obviously both mental and physical. *He murdered his girlfriend before he died!*'

Holly felt faint. She sank down into a chair, her features the colour of watery concrete. 'Oh, my God!'

'You didn't notice anything amiss with him before you went out?'

'No, I barely glanced at the workmen. They made a mess of sinking the well, and came back to put it right. When I left they were . . . working. That's all, working.'

'I see.' The detective moved towards the door. 'Well, thank you, Mrs Mannion. If you don't mind, we'll just have a look round the site and the machinery – just a formality. Otherwise, you'll be hearing from us after your husband returns home. Good evening to you.'

By the time Holly was sufficiently recovered from her shock to get up from the chair and cross to the window, the policemen had left. Obviously they had found nothing out there to interest them. She was trembling as she stood there watching the setting sun sink slowly beyond the Bryn in the distance, the heather slopes a deep purple turning to black as the evening shadows crept in. Soon it would be night, and she felt afraid. Very much afraid.

Mike was gone, there was nobody else here, she was all alone until the workmen . . . *workman* arrived in the morning. Surely the older man would not turn up for work as usual, not after . . . *that*! She found herself wishing that she had gone to her mother's, after all. At least then she would not have been told tonight.

She turned the key in the door and checked that it was locked. As she turned back into the room she was aware of the pungent, rotting odour, that awful stench that had become so familiar this last couple of days. The window was closed but it still seeped in, coming in wafts like an intermittent breeze, its foulness seemed to touch her like cold, clammy, stinking fingers. She shivered, threw another faggot on to the stove and leaned close to the iron firebox door so that she could inhale the sweet fumes of the woodsmoke. And when she straightened up the smell had gone.

It was the septic tank, she told herself over and over again until she was almost convinced. It needed emptying. Mike could arrange that as soon as he returned from London.

She switched on the light, deciding there and then that she would leave it on all night. Because somehow that malignant stench and the blackness of night seemed to complement each other.

Jim Fitzpatrick turned up for work at Garth Cottage at nine o'clock the following morning. Holly watched from the window as he drove the Land Rover down to the hollow where the well was, got out and began mixing some cement with no hesitation. He looked exactly as he had done yesterday and the day before: surly, workmanlike, a stolid servant of the well-drilling company. His mate had died, so he had to carry on, shoulder the extra workload. So emotionless, it was terrifying. No pity, no respect for the dead. It seemed as though he didn't care; a piece of human machinery was broken, so he carried on without it until he could find a suitable replacement.

It was as hot as ever today, not so much as a wisp of cirrus cloud in the unbroken gun-blue of the sky. Sweltering. Holly risked opening the kitchen window and took a cautious breath. That smell was gone, thank God! All the same she decided, she was going to remain indoors today. All day. Maybe she would begin decorating the lounge, take off all that plaster that had not already fallen off. At least it would be something to do, but it was no good trying to pretend that it would take her mind off things because it wouldn't. Nothing would. That boy was dead, a youth not yet in the prime of his life, sick and crazed. A murderer! And he had seemed so nice, so respectful. It was unbelievable.

The plaster on the lounge wall fell off in huge shards with just a touch from the trowel. In less than an hour the bare cementwork was exposed, reminding her of an undulating 3-D wall map, with contours and valleys that needed to be filled in. She wondered if Bennion's man had any spare cement; if so, he might even mix up a bucketful for her. She hesitated, not just because he seemed so surly but because she didn't like going outside. That youth, Eaton, had been out there yesterday, working like a normal person. Within hours he had become a murderer and had died of some terrible illness. But, she told herself, this place could not possibly have anything to do with it; he might have undergone the same fate if he had been on a job in the town. He *would* have.

The door was still locked from the previous evening. And the kitchen light was still burning. She switched off the fluorescent strip, unlocked the door and stepped outside, then caught her breath sharply. *The smell was back again, just a faint hint of it in the hot, windless atmosphere!*

Definitely the septic tank! She tried to ignore it as she looked for Jim Fitzpatrick. He was sitting in the Land Rover; just sitting, neither eating his 'bait' nor reading his daily paper. Staring fixedly. *At Holly!*

She tensed, feeling embarrassment and unease. All right, she knew all men looked at women, fantasized. But this labourer was so crude – there was no other word to describe him. A fish and chips and beer man, a glutton and a drunkard, she decided. Perhaps she was being unfair to him. She had hardly spoken to him during the whole time he had been working here, but she sensed his resentment towards her and Mike. An old-fashioned class hatred because they could afford a well and he was being paid just a basic wage to install it. Now he was eyeing her lustfully.

She swallowed, and changed her mind about the cement. She could fetch some from town – an hour or two away from the Garth would do her good. Just as she was turning away to go back indoors he spoke to her through the open Land Rover vehicle.

'Can I 'elp you, missus?'

'I wanted some cement, just half a bucketful to patch up the lounge wall.' Now that was a damned fool thing to say, she told herself, but the words had just seemed to spill out. She stepped back a pace, knowing that she was blushing deeply.

'I reckon I can fix that,' he leered, unlatching the door so that it creaked open and gave her an unrestricted view of his unbuttoned shirt front with a bulging roll of grimed fat hanging over the waistband of his working trousers. 'And, come to think of it, there's sommat you can do for me as well!'

She nearly screamed '*no*' and would have fled if her feet had not appeared to be stuck firmly to the ground beneath her. Instead she asked in a shaking voice. 'What do you want?'

'Some water to drink. It's hot out here and I ain't riskin' that well water, not until it's been passed clear.'

'All right. I'll get you some.' Her feet could move now, and she began retracing her steps back to the doorway.

Suddenly she realized that he was following her. She glanced back quickly and saw him shambling after her like a gorilla dressed in filthy human workclothes; dragging his feet, head hung low, long arms swinging at his sides. Oh, God! She thought about running, dashing indoors, slamming and locking the door. Phoning the police.

Don't be silly, she thought. He's only coming for a drink of water. You said you'd get him one, and he can hardly expect you to wait on him, bring it to the Land Rover on a tray and stand there whilst he drinks it. But he's not coming indoors!

Jim Fitzpatrick did come indoors. He appeared not to notice the hint as Holly let the door swing to behind her. He eased his bulky frame inside and lowered it down on to a chair at the table, breathing heavily, his chest wheezing. Fags, she surmised, he's probably a sixty-a-day man – and who could blame him when he had to work in stenches like the one out there. He closed his eyes briefly, then opened them again.

'Ta!' He took the mug of water, drank half of it at one gulp, puffed out his cheeks and gave her another leer. 'It's a bloody killer today. Must be getting on for ninety out there.'

'Yes, it's hot.' She wished that he would hurry up and drink the rest and leave.

'Your hubby's gone off for the day, 'as 'e?'

'He might be back at any time.' She was glancing about her, and eyed the breadknife still on the board – a potentially lethal weapon with crumbs adhering to its serrated blade. 'He shouldn't be long. I'm terribly sorry to hear about your mate.'

'Tommy? Shame, ain't it? 'E wasn't well yesterday, but you can't just go knockin' off 'cause you're off the 'ooks, can you? If you ask me, it was one o' them brain tumours, been brewin' up maybe for months and suddenly came to a 'ead. Sent 'im berserk, the cops reckon. Strangled his wench, and then whatever was growin' on 'im bursted and spewed all up the walls. Still, life 'as to go on, don't it? I just 'ope the gaffer sends me another bloke afore too long, 'cause this is bleedin' 'eavy work all on yer tod.'

Holly felt sick with revulsion. All this man thought about was a replacement; mates were dispensable. He took another drink and set the mug down on the table. And it was then that she noticed his lower lip and felt bile scorching her throat. Oh, God, it was awful. Revolting!

A sore or a boil – some kind of ulcer, anyway. It protruded from the soft lip, as big as a marble, shiny with the yellow matter that seeped out of it in a sluggish trickle down on to the stubbly, dirty chin. He seemed oblivious of it, and just stared at her.

'Is your hubby likely to stop away overnight?' It was a low whisper, a husky grating sound that was loaded with lust. Red-eyed as though he had not slept last night, his features were burning with some fever beneath the oil streaks and grime.

'Why?' Now that's a stupid bloody question if ever there was one, she realized.

'Must get a bit creepy out 'ere on yer own.' A low guffaw stuck in his throat. 'I mean, there ain't another 'ouse close by, and what with that awful bloody smell out there, it's enough to frighten any pretty young girl, ain't it?'

'I don't mind.' She was shaking. She glanced at the door, but he was between her and a dash to safety; she was sure that she could outrun him in the open, he was so ungainly, lumbering. 'Anyway, Mike should be back before long.' He won't come back for another couple of days, and this fellow sensed it, she decided. Her thoughts returned to young Tommy: what had happened to him, what he'd *done*. 'I'm expecting a visitor shortly, anyway.' The lie seemed more feasible.

'Yer fancy bloke comin' round, is 'e? A bit on the side, eh? Yer knows what they say, when the cat's away. . . .'

'How dare you!' She was so indignant at this innuendo, anger overcame her fear for a moment. 'I wouldn't sleep with any man except my husband, I'll have you know!'

'They all say that,' he grinned, slobbering some more of that vile matter, and Holly thought she saw another of those dreadful sores on his tongue. She jerked her head away and thought that she might throw up.

'Would you leave, please?' She spoke unconvincingly, staring at the wall – could not bear to look at him again. Everything connected with Garth Cottage had become a nightmare.

'All in good time.' He was noisily slurping the remains of his drink. 'I'll 'ave some more water, if you'd be so kind.'

No! Get it yourself, help yourself to anything you want, but just let me out of here, she thought.

He was struggling up on to his feet, breathing noisily. *Coming after her!* She thought again about the bread-knife, but it was on the table, nearer to him than to herself. *Oh, Merciful God!*

'Somebody's comin'!' There was both alarm and annoyance in his voice. She looked round and saw that he was staring in the direction of the partially open door. Sure enough, soft footsteps padded across the ground outside and scuffed on the dusty patio. There was a faint whiff of that smell but it was gone as quickly as it had come, maybe just a memory that lingered to plague her.

Whoever it was had stopped outside the door, waiting there as though uncertain whether or not to knock before entering. Holly saw a shadow slanting in through the gap, a figure clutching a bag of some kind. Waiting.

'Come in.' There was relief in her voice, a release of pent-up tension. Oh, *please*, come in, she prayed. Whoever you are, I need you!

'Hi!' The familiar figure of Nick Paton, the plumber, was framed in the doorway, his tool bag in one hand, his eyes flicking from Fitzpatrick to Holly. 'Thought I smelled the kettle. Just in time, am I?'

'He's. . . .' Holly couldn't remember Fitzpatrick's name, didn't want to, just wanted him out of the house. 'Our friend's just about to leave. He's hoping to finish the job this afternoon so that he won't have to come back tomorrow.'

'You'll be lucky.' Jim Fitzpatrick could not conceal his disappointment at this unexpected interruption. 'Not unless the gaffer sends me a mate in the next hour. I'll need the electrician to connect the pump back up. Young Tommy could've done that, but 'e ain't around, is 'e?' Then he was shuffling through the door, dragging it shut behind him.

'Grumpy old sod, is Jim.' Paton placed his bag on the floor. 'Got a chip on his shoulder, but a heart of gold really. Bennion rang and asked me to pop down. There's been some trouble. . . .'

'I heard about it.' Holly was filling the teapot, splashing some of the boiling water because her hand was shaking.

'Bad show, that.' Nick shook his head. 'But we don't know any details, they're not telling us a lot. Anyway, the old man wants to get this job finished as soon as possible. There's a fellow over at Cemmes screaming out to have his well started. I'll fix the pump and make sure everything's working. Then you'll be rid of us for a bit.'

'For a *bit*!'

'Well, we can't cement the liner in and remove the waste pipe until you've had your water passed pure, can we?' Nick sipped his tea. 'Who knows, we might have to fetch the lot up again if this doesn't do the trick!'

'Mike's gone to London for a couple of days.' Now why am I telling that to the plumber? she wondered. Because I don't want to be left here alone with that awful man.

'I'll be around.' Maybe Nick Paton sensed what had happened. 'I want to try and get my part of it finished tonight, if possible. You don't mind if I work late, do you?'

'No, not at all.' Holly felt weak with relief and sat down.

'One thing, that stink's gone,' the plumber said. 'Not a niff out there. It must've been the surface pollution, and now it's all drained away. That's a relief.'

'A big relief,' Holly sighed, and tried to push the memory of those revolting sores on Jim Fitzpatrick's mouth out of her mind.

She told herself that they were probably only enlarged mouth ulcers. She was letting her imagination run riot.

8

Nick was still working up in the loft. Holly could hear him using the electric drill from time to time. Then he went back outside and was doing something with the pump until almost dark, when he went back to the attic. She heard a gurgling of water. It was running freely somewhere, and it sounded as if the header tank might be filling. Under normal circumstances she would have been euphoric at the thought of having water again, but things were far from normal. The water had come from down *there*; she shuddered – where that foul smell came from. Anyway, it wouldn't be drinkable, at least not until Bill Kemp had called and given it the all clear. Even then, she wondered if she could bring herself to touch it.

She had spent the evening in the lounge, stripping the other wall. The furling paper came off easily, a sure sign of rising damp, but the wall underneath it was nowhere near as bad as the end one. She thought she might even be able to put a new roll of wallpaper straight on it.

She had gone off the idea of cementing the other wall. In all probability she would make a terrible hash of it, anyway. There was a roll of wallpaper under the bed upstairs, awaiting this job when eventually she got round to it. Tired as she was, the time seemed appropriate. She would not sleep tonight, that was a certainty, and she decided it was better to do something than lie awake letting her imagination run riot.

'That's it, then.'

The door opened, making her jump. A moment of fear, and then relief as she saw Nick's now familiar sheepish grin. 'All finished. You're plumbed in. Just turn on the taps and you'll have as much water as you're ever likely to need.'

'Except that it's contaminated.'

'True, but you can wash clothes in it. Or bath in it.'

'Ugh!' She was thinking of the stench, Tommy Eaton's unfortunate fate, his girlfriend's murder. All related, she felt sure. The water would leave its vile smell on her body, a terrible reminder of recent happenings.

'There's no smell now,' he assured her. 'In fact, if I didn't know about the failed test I'd probably drink it quite happily.'

'I think we'll wait until the water inspector's tested it again,' she smiled.

'Doing some decorating?' He moved into the room; he did not seem to be in any hurry to go home. 'That wall's in a right mess. Whoever plastered that in the first place wants shooting.'

'I was thinking about cementing it up,' she replied. 'I would have done, except that I didn't have any cement.'

'Cement's no good.' He shook his head. 'Those rough places want replastering and the cracks filling in with tetrion.'

'Oh!' She was dismayed because plastering was a skilled job. It meant finding somebody to do it and hanging about waiting for them to come; meantime, the decorating came to a standstill.

'I'll do it for you,' he said.

'Oh! Well, that's awfully sweet of you, Nick. When can you fit it in?' Three weeks, perhaps a month, she guessed.

'I'll do it for you now. I've got some plaster and tetrion in the van. Shouldn't take long – a couple of hours, maybe. Then you'll have to let it dry for a couple of weeks before you paint over it.'

She glanced at her watch. 'But it's a quarter past ten.'

'No matter. Hang on, I'll go and get what I need out of the van. And I wouldn't mind another cuppa before I start.'

'Fine. And whilst you're plastering, I'll start putting the paper on the other wall. First things first – let's see if that kettle's boiling on the stove.'

They worked steadily, Holly struggling with the wallpaper, Nick seeming to skim the wall effortlessly, stopping every so often to mix up some more plaster. Both of them kept the conversation away from Tommy Eaton; it would be in the papers for weeks to come, doubtless.

'Blimey!' Nick was kneeling by the bucket, stirring his latest mix with a stick. 'Phew!'

'What is it?' Holly was unable to look round as she struggled with head-height wallpaper and smoothed out a ripple.

'That bloody smell again!'

'It must be in the water you're mixing with. See, I told you. Even this resealing job isn't going to get rid of it.'

'It's gone again now.' He shook his head in bewilderment. 'Funny how it comes and goes. But, in any case, you'll have to pump the well to waste for several days to get rid of it altogether. Never mind, it won't affect the plaster.'

Holly felt goosepimples on her stretched arms. She saw once again Jim Fitzpatrick with that ulcer on his bottom lip, its pus trickling down his chin, another sore on his tongue. Don't think about it, she told herself. It *can't* be anything to do with the water. He's a heavy smoker – more likely it's mouth cancer.'

'That's about it.' Nick Paton dropped the trowel back into his empty bucket and stood admiring his handiwork.

Superb, he reckoned. A plasterer could not have done any better.

'It's marvellous.' Holly was almost finished, too. 'Oh, Nick, I can't thank you enough. You've no idea how grateful I am.'

Her pouted lips were homing in on his oily cheek, an intended peck of gratitude. Nothing more. But suddenly it was so very different. The casual, shy young plumber's head moved sideways and upwards, his lips were elevated, and drew hers like a magnet. Warm and soft, touching, brushing; then crushing together. Her arms went up and around his neck and held him close. His encircled her waist, and she could feel her breasts pressing against his chest.

'Oh, Nick!' He was still holding her. Their eyes met. For a few seconds everything else was forgotten – the borehole, the deaths, even the decorating. Two people had kissed, and everything had changed. It was unbelievable – Holly's brain was spinning, and she heard herself say, 'Kiss me again, Nick. *Please*.'

Still holding on to each other, they made their way back into the kitchen, this time heading for the sagging old Chesterfield settee that would cost a fortune to renovate and would probably stay as it was until it fell to pieces. Sinking down on to it, Holly lying underneath this previously shy young man, opening her mouth for him to thrust his tongue inside in a simulation of what her body was screaming out for.

She closed her eyes as she felt his rough fingers struggling with the waistband of her denim shorts, lifted herself up so that he could pull them down, kicked them free and still kept her eyes closed, waiting for the ultimate result of what was meant to be just a friendly kiss. *I don't want to see, I might change my mind.* She knew she wouldn't; it was too late now anyway. He was inexperienced, a workaholic who was perhaps discovering a new delight, and she had to help him find her, pushing hard at him and gasping her pleasure aloud. The old settee creaked its protest, its springs squeaking as they struggled to keep time with the lovers.

For Holly it was over too quickly. Nick was reaching for his discarded garments almost guiltily, afraid to look at her, perhaps fearful of a rejection even though it was too late. She lay there, naked from her ruffled T-shirt downwards, thighs wide and willing him to look. But he did not. He was Nick the plumber again, checking his tool bag, picking up his bucket and trowel, shuffling towards the back door.

'I'll be on my way, then.' Which was exactly what he had said when he had finished work the last time.

'Why don't you stop the night, Nick?' She was almost pleading.

He hesitated, and for one second she thought, hoped, that he was going to agree. Then he shook his head slowly, still not looking at her. 'No. Thanks all the same. I've got to be up and out early tomorrow. The jobs are piling up whilst Bennion keeps calling on me. Thanks all the same, though.'

'Goodnight, Nick.' Holly was unable to disguise her disappointment.

'Goodnight.' She wished he would call her by her name, but he was too shy, embarrassed now. It could well have been his first time.

'Nick?'

'Yes?' He was in the doorway. He stopped but did not look back.

'If you change your mind on the way home, come back. I'd be very happy if you did.'

She saw the back of his head nod, and then he was gone out into the night. A couple of minutes later she heard the Escort's engine turn over two or three times, then fire. Then he was gone. But he might return – she clung wildly to that forlorn hope. Oh, God, it had been wonderful! Maybe a minute of ecstasy that had left her in limbo, and she was likely to remain there for some time! It was crazy, though; she had not even *fancied* him before that kiss, which was only meant to be a friendly peck, anyway. It was as though something had come over her, robbed her of every vestige of self-control.

A feeling of guilt threatened but she pushed it away. What was done was done, and she would happily do it again. She lay there with her eyes closed, reliving those sensual seconds, trying to will an orgasm, but it hovered beyond her reach. Oh, Nick, *please* come back, she thought. I'm lying here waiting for you.

Time was suspended. She wanted this night to go on forever. She wondered how long Mike was likely to be away. His meeting was tomorrow; there would be a lengthy lunch, then another discussion with his agent. Bob would probably take him out to dinner, perhaps a show afterwards. No, Mike would not return tomorrow. A short time ago she had been desperate for her husband to come back; now she wanted him to stay away. Which was pointless, because Nick didn't have to return to Garth Cottage – the job was finished. Unless . . . she thought about phoning the plumber, inventing some reason, some difficulty with the new water supply. 'Nick, I don't understand how the various stopcocks work, you did explain but I've forgotten. Come and show me again. Tonight.'

Somewhere amid her erotic dreams she heard footsteps outside. Her imagination, doubtless, hearing him again, a fantasy in which he would return and make her orgasm this time. She pulled her T-shirt right up above her breasts and lay there listening. I'm ready, Nick, she thought. I've never been anything else. Come on in and make me finish.

The door was starting to open, scraping back across the uneven quarried floor. A breath of warm night air engulfed her sweating near naked body, bringing with it the odour of putrefaction. Which was why she sat up suddenly, pulled her T-shirt down and looked for her shorts. She turned her head in anticipation of seeing the plumber shyly hanging back on the threshold, waiting for her to summon him. Then screamed as she recognized her nocturnal visitor.

It was Jim Fitzpatrick!

There was no mistaking Frank Bennion's workman. It could not be anybody else, even though his swarthy features had changed and were a mass of those swollen, weeping sores. The original one on his lower lip would surely burst at any second, she thought. It had come to a bulbous head and was straining with the pressure of the stinking matter that dribbled from it. His eyes were puffed up and virtually closed, and he could surely see almost nothing. Mucus bubbled out of his nostrils, congealing. He was pitiful and horrible. Only then did she notice his clothing, and recoiled at the sight of those oily overalls now saturated with blood, fresh and dripping on to the floor, his hands slippery with the scarlet fluid as he clasped them to his disfigured face and moaned in anguish.

'Help me. Help me!'

She managed to rise to her feet, backed away, glanced at the wall phone and wondered if she might have time. Certainly Fitzpatrick, in spite of his terrible appearance, seemed weak and almost on the verge of collapse. Gone was the lusting leer, in its place a mask of diseased mental and physical agony.

She made it as far as the telephone, hesitated to grab the receiver and asked in a shaking voice, 'What . . . what's happened?'

'I . . . I've *murdered them*!'

'Who?' For God's sake, *who*?'

He was sobbing, his words barely audible, festered lips moving, eyes shedding uncontrollable tears which caught in the thick yellow poisoned liquid. 'The missus . . . the kids . . . I've killed them!' It was meant to be a scream, but it came out as a strangled grunt, then died away. He just stood there, pathetic and awful, bowed. Asking her for help.

'What do you want me to do?' What *can* I do? she thought.

'*Kill me*!'

'*Oh, my God*! The breadknife was still on the table and she found herself staring at it. That was stupid, she told herself. She wouldn't kill him, she wouldn't know how, anyway. In any case, he looked close to death. Maybe any second he would sink down to the floor and just pass away. And, Christ, he stank abominably; he had the very same smell that had plagued her these past few days. *As if he had crawled right up out of that evil well outside!*

'I'll call an ambulance.' She took the receiver off the hook, her fingers groping for the dial. They were shaking too much, she would never manage it.

'*No!*' He lurched forward, hit the table, sprawled across it, then somehow levered himself back up on to his feet. *And to Holly's horror she saw that Jim Fitzpatrick had the serrated knife clasped in his bloodied hand!*

Miraculously she did not panic. She knew that the telephone was her only chance, she had to summon help. A trembling finger found the right digit, dialled 9 . . . 9. . . . *Oh, please* . . .9. She heard it ringing out almost instantaneously. *Oh, hurry!*

Not wanting to look, she closed her eyes. I've done what I can, she thought. I can't do any more. She could hear him breathing, a kind of snorting sound. Any second he would be upon her, that blade plunging deep into her. Twisting, gouging.

'*Which service do you require?*' A voice so far away, too far to help her. Holly tried to speak, but all that came out was an incoherent whisper.

There was a moment of silence, and she could not even hear Fitzpatrick wheezing in his diseased lungs. Perhaps he was already dead. No, if he was, she would have heard him fall to the floor.

'*Which service do you require?*' The voice was more insistent, even angry, in case it was a hoax.

Then there was a noise like water gushing, like the waste pipe pumping the well to try to clear it. No, that wasn't quite right. . . . Still she did not dare to look. Now it was a hissing spray; a trickling.

The voice came on the other end of the line again, sharper, demanding.

'Ambulance.' Holly managed to get the word out and heard the call being transferred. Ambulance. For him or me? she wondered. It might be too late. She might be dying, or even dead before it came.

Something metallic clattered to the floor. That was when she opened her eyes and stared aghast. She didn't scream – she was done with screaming now – just looked, and tried to take the scene in. It took several seconds for it to register.

Fitzpatrick was standing away from the table, a grotesque caricature soaked in blood and pus. His eyes were closed, retracted into their swollen, ulcerated sockets; his disfigured lips pressed tightly together, forcing the poison out of those dreadful sores; his long arms extended in an almost pleading gesture, palms uppermost, sleeves pulled up to reveal a wide gash on each wrist from which blood spurted, jetted up and sprayed the ceiling, mottling it crimson. Twin claret fountains, gathering force, arced so that they splashed the walls. There was blood everywhere, and still more blood.

In some inexplicable way it was a relief for Holly, and when the crackling voice spoke in her ear again she was able to answer: name, address, directions to Garth Cottage. It all took time, and when she was finished Jim Fitzpatrick had buckled to the floor and rolled over on to his back, arms splayed, the force of the blood from his slashed wrists beginning to slow.

9

Holly was surprised how calm she was, though shaken. She was able to answer the questions put to her by the police. It was the CID detective who had called to question her about Tommy Eaton – Detective Sergeant Lewis, tall and sharp-featured. He showed consideration towards her and closed the door on the kitchen so that the forensic experts could go about their work.

'I've arranged to have the kitchen cleaned up for you when we're through, which should be in about a couple of hours or so,' he smiled kindly. 'A straightforward case of suicide, I think. But it's his *condition* which worries me. He's got some awful sores on his body.'

'Like Tommy Eaton's?' Holly watched carefully for a reaction.

'Yes.' Lewis was tight-lipped, noncommittal. 'We're awaiting the results of tests on those. I understand your husband is still away. Surely you're not going to remain here alone until he returns?'

She experienced a sinking feeling, a sensation of dread. Was this policeman trying to warn her of something – something which he was not allowed to talk about? 'I'll probably go to my mother's,' she lied. That was the last place she wanted to go.

'Have you telephoned your husband?'

'No. I've only got his agent's office number, and they won't be there at this hour.'

'But, surely, in an emergency . . .'

'There's no emergency, is there?' She averted her eyes from his penetrating gaze. 'A man has slashed his wrists in our kitchen, but it doesn't *involve* us. Does it?'

'No, not directly.' He seemed surprised. 'Obviously, we have to question, as we did over the Eaton boy, but after that it's no concern of yours. We would just like a word with your husband, though, when he returns. Routine. Now, if you'll excuse me, I must go and assist the others in the kitchen. If you want to leave, please carry on.'

'Thank you, sergeant. But I think I'll have a bath first.' She felt a need to cleanse her body, to wash this night's filth off herself.

It seemed strange to be turning on the bath taps again after several weeks of washing in water carried up from the village in containers. There was certainly a good pressure – the water was jetting out with force. She tipped some foam into it and went through to the bedroom to take her clothes off. Downstairs she could hear the distant, incessant mutter of police voices. Their presence gave her comfort but she knew that once they left, the terror would roll back. She would sit listening for footsteps outside in the dark night, anticipating a tap on the door. Eaton and Fitzpatrick were both dead; who else could possibly call round in that physical state? She did not want to think about it.

She lowered herself into the frothy bath foam, lay back and relaxed. For the moment she was safe, but she had to find a refuge for this night which was already well advanced. One could not very well go calling on neighbours at three in the morning. And then her thoughts suddenly switched to Nick Paton and the pleasure which had preceded the horror. She felt herself tremble at the thought of him and what had happened. Nick would understand; she would phone him, fetch him out of bed and talk to him. Oh, yes, she would do just that the moment she had dried herself.

There was no hurry. Another five minutes relaxing in this beautiful bath would make no difference to her plans. She sat up, reached for the hot tap and turned it on. A little too hot, she decided. It needed cooling down a degree or two. The cold tap spurted with force, and in that instant she was leaping out, slopping foaming water all over the bare, unvarnished floorboards, just managing to check a scream. *For the tap water was a filthy brown which reminded her of that slurry which the rig had pumped out like liquid excrement, with bits floating and swirling amid the foam.*

She stood looking at it, heaving even as she smelled it, the same stench of putrefaction which had lingered in the atmosphere outside and permeated the house. The smell of rotting evil, the odour of . . . *death and weeping, festering sores that consumed body and mind*!

Holly rushed from the bathroom, slammed the door behind her and wished that the bolt had been on the outside. *Ugh!* Standing there dripping in the bedroom, she examined her naked body in front of the tall wardrobe mirror. Thank God, she did not have any of those cancerous growths on her flesh! Yet.

She dried herself with trembling hands and hurried to dress, her blouse and jeans trying to resist her damp skin. *Christ, I have to get away from here! Now.* She would go downstairs and phone Nick, she decided. Damn it, she couldn't, the telephone was in the kitchen and the police were still working in there.

To hell with phoning – just go, she told herself. When you've seduced somebody a matter of hours ago, you didn't stand on ceremony. 'I've come round for you to screw me again, Nick.' At least that would take her mind off everything else.

She was surprised to see a light still burning in one of the lower windows of Nick's renovated cottage as she drew into the drive and parked behind his van. She suddenly felt uneasy, guilty; it was something of an imposition to arrive unannounced at three-fifteen a.m.

'Oh, it's *you*!' He must have heard her arrival. He stood framed in the doorway, a tousled, pallid figure still wearing his grubby working shirt. He stared at her. 'Christ Almighty, you look about how I feel!'

There was something odd about him, she decided. His cheeks were hollowed, his eyes sunken, his face flushed in the porch light. 'Are you sure you're all right, Nick?'

'I'm okay.' He closed the door behind her. 'Just a bit off the hooks, as they say in the Midlands. Been overdoing it, I suppose. No good going to bed, because I wouldn't be able to sleep.'

Holly was studying him carefully, searching for a sign of one of those awful bloated . . . thank goodness, he seemed all right in that respect. Briefly she told him of the night's happenings, and saw him pale still further.

'There's some sort of disease going about.' He spoke in a hushed voice. 'Like Aids, if you know what I mean. Only worse. It ain't natural.'

'You should have seen what came out of my bath taps.' She closed her eyes briefly. 'Thick brown sludge with bits of . . . *something* floating in it!'

'Oh, I shouldn't worry about *that*.' He smiled weakly. 'That's what was left in the tank. A thought crossed my mind when I got home and I nearly gave you a ring. One thing I forgot to do was to clean out the two tanks in the loft. I'll call round tomorrow evening and put that right.'

'Thanks.' She managed to smile back. 'I don't think I've ever got out of the bath so fast in my life before. Nick, I'm certain that all this trouble with the borehole, that vile smell, is related to what has happened.'

'I don't think so.' He shook his head. 'Water is water. You might get salmonella and other diseases, like they get cholera abroad, but nothing like those two fellers had. If you ask me, they've picked it up from somewhere else – maybe been doing something they hadn't ought to be doing, if you get me. No, it won't be anything to do with the well.'

'I just hope you're right.' Her hand crept across and found his, and she caught her breath at her own daring. I must be crazy, she thought. I vamped him earlier, and now I've got the feeling again. She made a token effort to fight it off but it was growing stronger, a driving urge that had her leaning against him, her other hand resting on his thigh, moving stealthily along it, her slim fingers searching for something beneath the denim material; finding it, stroking it, feeling it respond. She glanced slyly up at his face; his eyes were closed and he was breathing quickly. Christ, she grinned to herself, here we go again – and I can't wait. I'm like a bloody whore. If it wasn't Nick it would be somebody else, I just can't help myself!

His zip was snagging, and he helped her to pull it down. She stroked his pulsing male flesh with one hand

and tugged at his waistband with the other. Now it was sheer desperation on both sides to get their clothes off. She guided his rough fingers where she wanted them, helping him because his inexperience was more evident now. Eagerness on his part excited her, was building her up to fever pitch; pushing him down on to the sofa, she clambered astride him. Rarely in her life had she been totally uninhibited as she was now: brazen, flaunting herself, easing her body off his and commanding him to look at her, doing things for him to see which she had never shown any man before, not even her husband. Euphoric because his tired eyes stared in amazement and excitement, she cried her pleasure aloud, breathing crudities which had never passed her soft lips before. Then going back down on to him she rode him frenziedly until they were both spent.

It was full daylight, and the rays of the early morning sun were slanting in through the window when Holly stirred. Her first awareness was of a slight headache, like the hangover a glass of whisky at a party gave her the following day. Squinting in the bright light, she was trying to remember. Then sat upright, aghast when everything came back to her. Nick, Fitzpatrick, Nick again. *Oh, God, I must have dreamed it all.* But she hadn't, because their clothes were still strewn around the sofa. Ashamed, she hurriedly retrieved her scattered garments and dressed. Only then did she shake her companion with a hand that trembled uncontrollably.

'Nick, wake up!'

He stirred, muttered something, and she shook him again. This time his eyes flickered open. They were glazed, as if he had cataracts, and he seemed to have difficulty focusing. A groan escaped his lips. She felt his forehead: it was warm and sticky. He had a temperature, he was ill. *Oh, my God!*

'What's . . . the matter?' He closed his eyes again.

'Nick, it's me, Holly. Are you ill?'

This time he made an effort to move and reared up into a sitting position. Slowly his eyes cleared. 'I'll be okay.' He looked around the room slowly. 'Christ, my head's thumping. There's a bottle of paracetamols on the shelf somewhere.'

By the time she had found them he had his trousers on. She was eyeing his bare torso fearfully, but there was no sign of any break in the flesh. She let out her pent-up breath. At least it isn't . . . *that*! She crossed to the sink and filled a glass with water, but found herself shying away from it in case it was discoloured, with particles of filth floating in it. It wasn't, it was clear. Nick popped the tablets into his mouth and swallowed them.

'I'll be all right in a minute or two.' He leaned up against the units and dropped his gaze from hers, embarrassed, inhibited by the memories of last night.

She almost apologized, but it might have made it worse. Holly could not understand what had come over her. She had always enjoyed sex, but not on that scale – promiscuity gone berserk, as if she was totally out of control, forced to go along with her body because she was caught up in a fierce current. It was frightening, more so when it was over because she did not know when it might happen again. Then the telephone rang, jarring them both.

'I'd better let you get it.' She stopped halfway across the room.

'No.' He sat down again. 'Let it ring. It'll be Bennion. I'm not going out today. In fact, I'm going to spend the day catching up on my sleep. But I'll call round and clean those tanks for you this evening.'

Her skin goosepimpled. *Oh, no, I'll be out, I don't want it to happen again.* 'Thanks.' She made for the door. 'If by any chance I happen to be out, the key'll be under that slate by the door.'

She read disappointment in his expression and hurried up the drive to where her car was parked. Maybe it would be better if she was out when Nick arrived tonight. She did not trust herself any longer. It was as if suddenly something had power over her.

The police were gone, the kitchen had been cleaned up. In fact, she could almost have convinced herself that last night had just been a nightmare. The water in the bath would prove it had been reality, but she hurried on past the closed bathroom door and went into the bedroom to change. She would ask Nick to let the water out tonight when he came. Which meant she had every intention of being here. She trembled, tried to tell herself that she could leave a note, but knew she wouldn't.

She was aware that she had a slight headache, too. Perhaps it had just started; or she might have had it since waking and been too preoccupied with everything else to notice it. Like Nick, she was short of sleep, but there was no way she was committing her body to the mercy of this place with its lurking evil whilst she slept.

She made a phone call to Bill Kemp at the Environmental Health Department and arranged for him to come and test the water the following day. Not that it would be any good because undoubtedly it was contaminated; it would be company, though, for half an hour. And Mike might come home tomorrow.

'I'll be round towards midday, Mrs Mannion.' Kemp sounded sleepy; perhaps he, too, had had a disturbed night, she thought. 'Make sure you pump it to waste in the meantime, though, to clear anything that might still be in the well.'

'All right.' Her heart sank. That meant going down to the hollow where the borehole was and turning the stopcock. She would have to go up into the attic, lift the float-switch out and stop the water coming into the house. Waterless for another day, back to square one.

It was a job that had to be done, Holly decided over a cup of coffee, and the longer she put it off the worse it would be. It reminded her of her childhood, when she was fully convinced that a monster lurked in the shrubbery at the bottom of her parents' garden and she avoided that place at all costs. After weeks of shying away from the laurels and rhododendrons, one day she confided her fear to her parents. Her mother had taken her by the hand, literally dragged her down there and poked in the bushes just to prove to her daughter that there was no bogeyman lurking there. After that she had not been scared any more. The only difference now was that she had nobody to accompany her. She could wait until Nick Paton came this evening. . . . No, she would go now, this very minute. Alone. Just as she had come back alone to Garth Cottage this morning.

Bright sunlight, no sinister shadows; she stood on the patio, looking down at the rough concrete square with its steel cover propped up on a large stone to allow the long blue waste pipe to snake out of it. Immediately below that manhole cover was a shaft going down into the depths of the earth, far into the stinking bowels of the Garth soil. Holly shivered in spite of the heat. Go on, get it over with, she urged herself.

She was trembling. Her legs didn't want her to go and threatened to throw her down on to the skimming of sun-baked slurry. Then she would have crawled back to the house, demoralized; defeated. She made a supreme effort, conscious of the beating of her heart, the roaring in her ears. Her headache was becoming perceptibly worse. *Go on, keep going.*

She made it to the top of the well, aware of the body odours which emanated from her. Shakily she knelt down, pulled the heavy metal to one side and dropped it to the ground. She stared at the top of that blue cylinder, saw the blackness that started a few inches down and jerked her eyes away. *No, I'm not going to look.* Just turn that stopcock and have done with it, she told herself.

The wheel was stiff. Or else her trembling fingers were weak. She grunted, and used both hands. It still would not give. Blast those fellows for turning it so tight, she thought. Didn't they realize that somebody else might have to release it?

It started to move, but hardly had she completed a quarter of a turn than she heard the noise coming from deep down the narrow well shaft. At first she thought it was water beginning to move, being pumped up. But it was no liquid sound, rather a harsh rasping that was rising in pitch. *A groan, one that embodied the ultimate in physical pain and mental anguish, conjured up in her tortured, frightened brain a vision of one who writhed and convulsed. She saw again Jim Fitzpatrick on the floor of the kitchen with his life's blood jetting up to the ceiling, and how Tommy Eaton might have looked when his flesh burst and splattered vile pus on the wall.*

A hiss of foul, diseased breath forced its way up the well liner, fetid air that hit her like a poisoned cloud and sent her reeling back, stumbling, fleeing blindly. But it pursued her, the stench enveloping her, seeping down into her lungs so that she retched and vomited down herself.

Dimly she was aware of water pumping somewhere with the force of a firefighter's hose being played on a raging inferno, hissing its fury in the field beyond the shrubbery. And she had no doubt in her terrified mind that the water would be dark brown with revolting contamination as the deep shaft spewed up the evil that it had spawned.

10

Mike Mannion woke with a throbbing headache and winced as the hotel room spun for a few seconds, then slowed, steadied. He groaned, not just because his head was pounding and his temples seemed to vibrate, but because there was something positively awful lurking in the recesses of his mind, waiting to manifest itself. Afraid of it, he wished that it would go away before he could remember what it was, and felt a desire to pull the sheets up over his head; to hide. Then it filtered slowly into his waking brain and he clutched the bedclothes into a tight ball with either hand. God, what a bloody fool he had been!

The meeting the day before and the deal on the book covers were temporarily pushed to one side. Last night superseded everything, and it was no good trying to pretend that it had not happened. Because it had.

He lay there trembling, eyes tightly shut as his memory plagued him. He could have caught the six-thirty train and been back at Garth Cottage by eleven at the latest. Instead, he had succumbed to the oldest, most powerful urge of all. If only Bob Daniels or John Farmer, the paperback company's art director, had invited him out to dinner none of this would have happened. But they had had prior engagements – the business was done as far as they were concerned. Mike had a cheque in his wallet, the contract signature money for the landscapes; everything was shaping up beyond his wildest dreams. And then he had to go and do a damned fool thing like that! *Jesus, I must be insane!*

It was all because he found himself with time on his hands in the big city. Wasn't there a saying that the devil found work for idle fingers? He had the opportunity to turn something which had been a fantasy for years into reality. The very thought had aroused him, fanning the flames of an erotic idea. A prostitute wasn't like an affair, you didn't get involved. You paid your money, had your fun, and that was that. Okay, there were risks, but it was exciting buying that packet of condoms from the dispensing machine in the toilets. Step one.

Step two was more difficult. How did you go about finding a whore? It was dangerous; you got hauled up into court if you approached an innocent woman. How then? He browsed through some books on a street bookstall and found himself looking at the sex mags which were kept out of reach. Those were no good to him, just posed models, hardly worth the couple of quid they were priced at, expensive fantasies – he had his own for free. But he wanted more than that. Then his eyes alighted on a magazine which seemed to be intent on hiding itself behind the others. A plain cover, nothing provocative, just the title – *Contacts*. A little shiver of excitement touched his spine. Christ, it was eight quid! So it had to be the real thing.

If Mike had not had that cheque in his pocket he might have thought twice about indulging in sordid erotic literature. But he bought it and quickened his pace back to his hotel room, where he scanned the pages with feverish excitement. Columns of offers, phone numbers. "Ring Cindy, I'm here to please." "Gents, relax and have a good time with Sandra, satisfaction guaranteed." His forefinger trembled as he got an outside line and started to dial. Hoping for a disconnected number, an engaged tone, he wanted to funk it now. Instead, he spoke to Joanna, husky-voiced but reluctant to chat. She gave him an address, said she would be free at nine and put the phone down. He took a cab.

Joanna had to be forty-five. Her face was thick with make-up, and her pungent perfume caught the back of his throat. He handed over three ten-pound notes and followed her up the stairs. Hell, his earlier erection had deserted him, and he was trembling as he watched her strip off. He registered a passable body with a sun-bed tan, and a bed with just a blanket spread out on it. She lay on it, waiting for him to finish undressing, and he detected an air of impatience about her, as if she was thinking, Time's money, and I've got someone else scheduled for nine-thirty.

He managed to revive his erection and rolled the rubber on. After that it was purely a case of thrusting away until it was all over. Joanna lay there impassively throughout, but smiled at him when he was done. That should have been the end of it; an expensive lesson, but nobody would be any the wiser. Except himself, haunted by shame and guilt in the aftermath of it.

Suddenly he leaped out of bed, stood naked in front of the tall mirror and examined his lower regions with fervent haste. Scrutinizing the flesh, he was looking for he knew not what. Pinker than usual, perhaps, but nothing untoward. It was all in the mind. That was the trouble!

He had checked out, paid his bill and phoned Holly. The first time there was no reply. Where the hell was she? Ten minutes later he got her, and thought how distracted she sounded. No, she insisted she was fine, there wasn't anything the matter; she'd meet him at the station at two-twenty. It was as if she knew, or guessed, what he had done, he thought. But that was crazy. All the same, it was going to be a difficult homecoming. He screwed up the contact magazine, thrust it deep into an overflowing street litter bin, glanced around in case anybody was watching, and almost ran to the station.

'Jesus Christ alive!' Mike stared aghast when Holly told him what had happened during his absence. 'Why didn't you phone me?'

Because then you would have had to come straight home, she thought. 'You couldn't have done anything.' She dropped her eyes, thought of Nick Paton and hoped her husband would not guess. 'The police want a word with you sometime, but I imagine there's no hurry. By the way, I called Mr Kemp. He came yesterday and took away another couple of samples. I had difficulty switching the waste pipe on to pump. . . .' Her voice tailed off.

'Why bother?' He was sullen. 'We can't stay here – that's a certain fact.'

'The excuse you've been looking for?' Hell, I want away, too, she thought, but it'll have to come from Mike.

'Excuses be buggered!' He was angry now. 'Two deaths, and all we've got is foul water.'

'We don't know, do we? Yet. Kemp said he'd phone; he'll try and get us an answer today. I rather think the authorities are as worried as we are. The police don't seem to connect it with the well.'

'There's no reason why it should be the well.' He wanted to reassure both of them. 'Something those fellows picked up, entirely unconnected with this place. Just a coincidence that they were working here.'

'You mean, like going with dirty women and catching something nasty?' She tried to laugh but it sounded forced.

'Don't be bloody stupid!' He almost shouted, and his features drained of their colour.

'All right, all right, there's no need to take it out on *me*!' She turned away. 'I'm glad everything went well for you. . . .'

The telephone interrupted her, screaming harshly at them, as if to say, Pack it up, you two!

'I'll get it.' He strode across the kitchen. It would either be the police or Kemp. It was Kemp.

'Afraid I've got bad news for you again, Mr Mannion.' The Environmental Health inspector sounded genuinely sorry. 'I'm afraid your water is still contaminated.'

'Bloody hell! How bad this time?' As if it mattered, he thought.

'A little improvement, but I'm afraid it isn't safe to drink. You seem to have got rid of the salmonella and animal matter. But there's still this other contamination, which we'll need a chemical test to identify.'

'I'm surprised, in view of recent happenings, it hasn't been done.' Mike was terse. 'I'd have thought it would have been the first step.'

'So far, nobody has requested it,' Kemp replied. 'And I can't authorize a test off my own bat. I'm afraid it's expensive.'

'I'll think about it,' Mike snapped.

'You do that,' Kemp said. 'But in the meantime I'd continue to pump the water to waste, if I were you. See if you can clear it. You never know.'

'I'm going to put this place on the market right now,' Mike said to Holly as he began thumbing through the yellow pages. He propped the directory on his knee until he found the heading which said 'estate agents'.

'You can't,' she said, and felt her stomach churning because she realized that she spoke the truth.

'Why not?' Defiant, he clutched the pages as if he meant to rip them through in a show of strength and anger.

'Nobody would buy it.' She walked over to the window and stood looking out. 'The only water we do have is contaminated. It's a buyer's market these days, that's why we came here. Before we can do anything, go anywhere, we have to get that water pure. When we've done that we *might* stand a chance. It's as simple as that.' She caught her breath, thinking she could smell that stench again, but then it was gone. It was preying on her mind.

'Then I'll ring Bennion.' Mike threw the directory on to the floor. 'It's his responsibility.' Even if he had lost two of his workmen? he asked himself. But it couldn't be anything to do with the borehole. Could it?

Mike was hiding something from her, she sensed it. A woman's intuition. But so was she hiding something from her husband. Nick Paton drifted back into her thoughts, and that was why she went outside and stood in the late afternoon sunshine.

There was definitely something down there; she could hear it, even when standing here on the patio. Like . . . earth tremors. No, that wasn't quite right, she decided. She didn't want to listen, but it was as if she was compelled to, despite telling herself it was all in the mind, her overstretched nerves. It was really the roar of the water still pumping to waste in Hughes' field beyond the shrubbery; the drone of a distant tractor; or the summer breeze rustling the shrivelled foliage. But she knew it was none of these. It was like a sighing that drifted up out of the well and was magnified at the top in the concrete pit, then escaped through the propped-up hatch with an angry hiss.

She sniffed the air fearfully, but there was only the sweet-sour smell of the drought, no freshness, no lushness. Like a world that was slowly dying, being poisoned.

'Bennion's coming round right away.' Mike's voice made her start and her heart flipped. She had not heard him come outside. 'Jumpy, aren't you?'

'Wouldn't you be if you'd been here alone the last couple of days?' She jerked her head away, and stiffened when he slipped an arm around her waist. 'I'm sorry, Mike. It's got on my nerves.'

'Of course it has.' He kissed the nape of her neck, and it was like some kind of guilt-burn making her writhe inwardly. 'I'm sorry, Holly.' For what I've done, he added silently. 'I must say, I didn't expect Bennion to come on the run. I imagine he wants his money, and knows very well I won't pay until the job's put right. In the meantime, we've just got to stick it out. Let's be practical; our only real problem is the contamination. Those deaths *can't* be anything to do with the well.'

'I suppose you're right,' she answered, and was glad when he let her go. Suddenly she didn't like him touching her. Because of Nick. Which was silly; nothing would come of her relationship with the plumber. She tried to convince herself of that, and it hurt.

'You could always go and stay at your mother's.'

'You know I'll never do that, Mike. No, there's only one thing for it – we have to see it through.'

Frank Bennion showed no outward sign of being perturbed by recent events. He looked fresh-faced and dapper, and the smile was back on his lips. His previous irritation had evaporated. He was a good businessman, Mike decided – he knew how to put on an act.

'I think I know what the trouble is.' Bennion strode down to the well, pulled the steel cover to one side, produced a torch and shone it down the liner. 'Yes, there's still a bit of a smell, but nothing like so bad as it was before.'

Mike and Holly had kept their distance; that square of concrete with its raised cover was like some awful snake pit from which a seething mass of deadly reptiles might wriggle to freedom at any second.

'Our fault, Mr Mannion.' Bennion straightened up. 'We rectified the leak of surface water by sealing the liner down to twenty feet. Which did the trick. But, of course, the existing bugs were still in there, weren't they?' He laughed as though to reassure his customers. 'All we have to do is to flush them out. A gallon of chlorine, pump to waste for a couple of days, and I'll *guarantee* the job this time. It was Fitzpatrick's fault, he forgot to clean out the well when he put the liner back.'

Holly felt a twinge of contempt for this man. His workman had died a horrible death before her own eyes and here was Bennion using him as a scapegoat. No mention of the tragedies; as far as he was concerned, they were over and done with, forgotten.

'We'll get that put right first thing in the morning.' Bennion glanced at his watch. 'I'll send somebody round to do it. Now, I must dash, I've got another appointment.'

'Always a bloody excuse.' Mike stood watching the BMW disappearing down the lane. 'But surely he's going to run out of excuses before long. Either that, or we'll have drinkable water eventually.'

Holly had been aware of the soreness at the base of her spine for the past few hours, like an adolescent spot that was screaming out to be squeezed. She rubbed it through her scanty underwear. It was quite sore, a kind of blind boil that had troubled her twice before in her life, the last time about ten years ago. It was an aggravation that made sitting down painful. She recalled the uncomfortable experience that resulted when she had visited her local GP. He had given her some tablets to bring it to a head, a nasty yellowish ulcer tinged with white. Then he had lanced it. Christ, it had hurt, and the stuff that he had got out of it stank enough to make her throw up. Every morning for a week she had had to go back to the doctor to have the dressing changed. Undignified, embarrassing, she walked with a shuffle and people in the street gave her strange sideways glances. Now the boil had returned, probably brought on by the stress of the last few days.

She went up to the bathroom, closed and bolted the door, and kicked her shorts off. God, you needed to be a bloody contortionist, she thought as, with the small mirror clasped in one hand behind her, she tried to view the sore area of her body. She pulled the top of the cheeks apart, noted a patch of skin that was slightly red and breathed a sigh of relief. At least it wasn't . . . don't think about it, she told herself. There was no head, and it might not even come to one. The first time it had just disappeared after a few days. She certainly wasn't going to the doctor to be put to all that discomfort again.

A sudden idea made her go back downstairs. She was relieved that there was no sign of Mike. He was probably working in his studio, she thought. She reached down a dog-eared book off the shelf in the kitchen; a sudden idea gave her a glimmer of hope. Flicking through the pages of homeopathic remedies. *Hepar sulph*. That had to be the one – anything was worth a try.

She recalled that there was a homeopathic chemist in town – she had bought some arnica from there once. She was sweating, trembling with relief; her mounting fear had been allayed. Tomorrow she would go and buy some hepar sulph; it might do the trick. But even if it didn't, then at least her sore wasn't one of . . . *those*.

11

It was after ten o'clock before Bill Cole arrived at Garth Cottage in the Land Rover. Holly was standing in the window, impatiently awaiting the arrival of Bennion's workforce, and had made up her mind half an hour ago that they were not going to come today.

Bill Cole was nearing retirement age, tall and lanky with stooped shoulders, and a shock of grey hair which was usually only combed at weekends. His features might have belonged to a mortician. He rarely smiled, principally because for most of his waking hours there was a cigarette stuck in the centre of his lips. He never removed it until it was finished, when it began to scorch his lips; if there was sufficient butt remaining to light the next, then he held the soggy, glowing, nicotine-saturated remains to the next cigarette. Otherwise he leaned forward, spat the end on to the ground and extinguished it beneath his working boot. His perpetual cough ensured that a frequent supply of ash showered down the front of his greasy blue overalls. He experienced equal difficulty in talking through his cigarette, and when he spoke he invariably coughed, so he said as little as possible.

He had worked for Frank Bennion for the last couple of years, ever since the quarry had closed down. Bennion had bought the rig and Bill had gone with it. A slow-thinking man, Bill Cole did not understand the technicalities of well-drilling; he just carried out instructions. A labourer, he was given the straightforward jobs. He knew that all he had to do here was to turn the pump off, pour a can of chlorine down the liner and set it pumping to waste. It was not quite as simple as it sounded, because the odds were that when he turned the stopcock nothing would happen – the pump would either continue to operate or else it wouldn't come back on when he wanted it to. The whole business was hit-and-miss, he decided, money for old rope, ripping off customers like these folks who had got bad water and weren't likely to get anything better.

'Good morning.'

He turned slowly and saw the attractive young woman coming down the well-trodden track towards him. He nodded, coughed and dislodged an inch of ash from his cigarette. His cough rumbled on, and he waited for it to subside before he spoke. 'Mornin'.' What else was there to say? Embarrassed, he wished that she had kept away and left him to do the job he had come here for.

'We're having a lot of trouble with the well.' Holly was not complaining directly, just stating a grievance. 'Do you normally have all this trouble getting wells right?'

'Depends,' he mumbled through his cigarette, and started off the cough again, a vibration in his lungs as if he was going to heave. 'Some work, some don't. The luck o' the draw. Trouble is' – he let his eyes rove furtively in case there might be an eavesdropper nearby – 'This lot's in too much of a bloody hurry to get on to the next job. Drill and 'ope, and 'ope again that we can put it right if it don't work. At the moment there's a gang of us followin' 'em round patchin' up, doin' what oughta bin done in the first place. No logic to it, it costs the firm more money than if they done the job right in the first place, if you understand me.'

'I do,' she smiled, thinking that she liked this simple labourer because he spoke the truth. 'It's been a night-mare, literally.' She paused, not wanting to broach the subject of Eaton and Fitzpatrick, just curious to know if it could be anything to do with this borehole.

'Them two, you mean?' He was whispering now, his words almost smothered by the continuous cough. 'Bloody 'orrible, by all accounts. Nobody knows what caused it. I 'ear they're still doin' tests and they've postponed the funerals. If you ask me, they oughta cremate 'em, burn whatever it is, get rid of it for good. Some kind o' brain cancer, the boss reckons. 'E says it's nothin' to do with the job. For once I agreed with 'im. I wouldn't be 'ere now if I thought otherwise. I mean, you ain't gonna catch a disease like that from *water*, are you?'

'No.' Holly was keeping her distance from the well. 'But it *has* been giving off a very nasty smell.'

'That'll be the surface contamination.' He reached in to the back of the Land Rover and dragged out a gallon can. 'See this stuff? Chlorine, it is – like they put in swimmin' baths to kill the germs. A gallon's far too much for this job, but it won't hurt, just cost the firm a bob or two extra.' He laughed, a low rumbling in his throat. 'But it'll kill any germs that are goin'. Now, I'd better get cracking. First I'll 'ave to turn the pump off. Perhaps you'd do it for me, just flick the switch in that box on the wall of the 'ouse, will you?'

'Would you like a cup of tea or coffee?'

'Not at the moment, ta.' He loosened the screw top on the can, grunting at the exertion necessary. 'But p'raps in about half an hour when I 'ave me bait.'

'I'll see to it.' Holly turned away, walked back towards the cottage, opened up the control box and depressed the switch. She heard the swish of water in the adjoining field stop almost immediately. 'I'll bring you one out in about half an hour,' she called.

She went back inside. If this latest ploy worked, then she would let Mike put Garth Cottage up for sale. The end of a short-lived era, the dashing of her hopes. Instinctively she felt at the sore place on her tail bone, winced and snatched her hand away. It was damnably painful; the sooner she went into town and got a homeopathic remedy, the better. There still wasn't anything more than a red patch showing on the skin, she had checked again this morning, using the hand mirror in conjunction with the dressing-table one and tilting the latter to give her an unrestricted view. After this fellow had fixed the borehole, she would take the car and fetch her hepar sulph.

Last night had been difficult. She had been forced to

sleep on her stomach, for what little sleep she had got. Mike had not slept much, either: she had been aware of him tossing restlessly. She knew him well enough to know when he had something on his mind. The meeting, the deal, had gone well enough, and for the first time for a long time they had some money – so what was bothering him? What had happened in between the official business?

'Are you sure you're okay, Mike?' she had asked around dawn, feeling that it was time one of them spoke.

'I'm fine.' He had not sounded convincing. 'Just restless. Overtired, I think. London never did suit me.'

Which, she realized, was as far as she was going to get. Her guilt was plaguing her. If it had just been a one-off adulterous relationship, maybe she could have lived with it. But it wasn't. She was experiencing an indescribable urge to see Nick again, excited by the memories of what had happened, desperate to mate with him again. It was a kind of carnal urge – nymphomania. She winced at the thought but it was true. Even in her present state of discomfort her thoughts were sexual ones, and she had never had a strong libido. Sex was something you did to please your man, she had always thought; she had never got wildly excited about it, as a lot of women did. She had not lost her virginity until she was twenty-two. Now all that had changed, and in the space of a couple of days she was craving for a man. One man – Nick Paton, the plumber. But she knew well enough that if it had not been for him then it would have been sombody else; her body was telling her that much. Once she found her fingers straying to sensuous parts, but she forced them away. This was no time to indulge in selfish delights; she was worried about Mike, what he had done in London. Hypocrite! Some time after dawn she had fallen into an uneasy doze.

Holly put the kettle on the stove. By the time it boiled, the workman outside would be just about ready for his 'bait'. Maybe she would take her own coffee out there and chat to him – for no other reason than that she was lonely, needed company, and Mike would not emerge from his studio until he felt like eating, which might not be until evening. Damn, she hadn't asked Bennion's man whether he preferred tea or coffee. She would have to give him a shout.

At that moment she heard the Land Rover start up, with a kind of frenzied urgency rather than the usual sluggish diesel noise to which she had become accustomed these past few days. She moved to the door and opened it. He was behind the wheel and the vehicle was starting to move. Perhaps he had finished the job, she thought, and was not going to stay for bait. It didn't really matter; she had no reason to run forward and shout to him.

His face turned in her direction, and she stopped, aghast, cold fingers clutching at her heart. There was a wildness in his eyes, his complexion was ashen and there was no sign of the perpetual cigarette in his mouth. The lips were moving; she could not hear him above the roar of the engine, but he was mouthing frantically at her. Behind the Land Rover she saw his tool bag, its contents strewn from the mouth of the well, an array of spanners and screwdrivers.

'Hey, you've forgotten your tools,' she yelled, feeling an urge to flee indoors, slam the door and lock it. She recoiled as her nostrils detected that awful stench of putrefaction, so strong that it was almost asphyxiating. Gasping for breath, she wanted to scream. *Oh, no, not again!*

'Get the hell out of here, like I'm doing!' She could hear him now; he had momentarily relaxed his foot on the throttle. '*Don't go near the well. Oh, Christ, it came right up at me! Run!*'

Helpless, trapped there in the hot summer sunshine, clawing with her hands as if to ward off an invisible fog that reeked of stinking evil, she tried to scream to him to help her, but he was already moving off, crashing the gears in his terror. The lumbering Land Rover shot forward and took an erratic course towards the gateway as the driver slumped over the wheel, trying to steer. There was a solid thump as the steel bumper clipped the gatepost, knocked it at an angle and scraped it with its tailboard on the way out. Like a roaring monster fleeing from some conflict, it skidded momentarily in the dry soil of the steep drive that led up to the lane.

'Wait!' Holly screamed after the departing Bill Cole. 'Come back!'

But he wasn't stopping, she knew that. Some awful manifestation, the stench its forerunner, had come up out of the borehole, angry and lusting to kill. Just as it had killed Tommy Eaton and Jimmy Fitzpatrick.

Holly Mannion was screaming hysterically now. Not just because of whatever had come up from out of the bowels of the foul earth but because she saw what was about to happen. She yelled a warning, knowing that it was futile, when she saw the speeding cement-mixer coming down the road, unwieldy, top-heavy, its barrel churning the concrete inside it.

Bill Cole had not seen the oncoming lorry, and he pulled right into its path, shooting forward into the road with surely no chance of avoiding a collision.

For Holly everything had slowed down like an agonizing slow-motion film. She found herself hoping that the mixer might miss the Land Rover. Or be able to pull up in time. It was so slow now that even if they crashed the impact would surely only be minimal.

The Land Rover had stalled, broadside across the lane; Bill Cole was frantically pumping the starter, totally oblivious of the onrushing wagon of death. The lorry driver was standing up in his cab, braking, wrenching at the steering wheel, shouting, cursing, screaming.

Impact! Steel met steel, and buckled; two vehicles became one as the wreckage crumpled together. Metal screamed its anguish and became unrecognizable scrap even as it lost momentum, slewed to a smoking, grinding halt and slowly toppled over and down the steep bank on the opposite side of the lane.

Sudden silence, and they were lost to view. It might never have happened. Holly tried to tell her tortured mind that it had not, that the Land Rover had surged on ahead of the braking lorry, that they were now out of sight, round the bend, continuing on their way, unscathed.

She did not want to see; far better to go back to the cottage and dial 999. Again. She told herself that it might not be as bad as she thought, that both drivers were already clambering out of their respective mangled vehicles, cursing each other, taking details down on scraps of paper – insurance companies, registrations.

She found herself listening, willing herself to hear voices, but there were none. Only silence, that same awful ominous stillness. She found her feet moving forward by themselves, defying her logical reaction to flee back to the cottage. Experiencing a kind of morbid fascination, she felt like a ghoul eager to view human carnage. Except that she did not want to look. But she had no choice.

She had lost all conception of time; it might have taken her hours or merely minutes to pass through the damaged gateway and up on to the road. The empty lane was strewn with fragments of broken glass, a piece of torn material lying amid the shatterings. Nothing else. Nothing. They've gone on their way; it never really happened, she thought. I don't need to look down that bank. *You do!*

Shying away, then forcing her frightened eyes to peer over, she saw the mountain of twisted metal, the mixer tipped over, its concrete oozing out like . . . slurry from the borehole! Something else caught her eye. She stared, recognizing the features instantly: the pallid complexion, the orbs wide with terror, the lips still mouthing their warning to her. *Run. Don't go near the borehole!*

Bill Cole, Bennion's labourer, his head upturned, was

looking at her from out of the long sun-browned grass. *And it was only when she moved forward to help him out of the ditch that Holly Mannion realized that there was no body attached to the ragged bloody neck!*

12

That old film was still running for Holly Mannion, a sequence of events which she was aware of, yet it was divorced from her. She did not remember screaming, fainting, or being helped up by Mike. For her it began when she was being assisted back to Garth Cottage, leaning on her husband, knowing that without his support she would have fallen. Content to be led, she nodded in reply to his frequent enquiries if she was all right. The events that had gone before were like a dream, and she could barely recall them. Shocked, numbed, she did not want to think for herself.

Mike took her into the kitchen, sat her gently on the settee and pushed her back into a lying position. He gave her a cup of tea, hot and strong, and two aspirins. She lay there wide-eyed, watching him as she drank the tea and swallowed the tablets with difficulty.

'My poor darling.' He sat beside her, his arm around her. From then onwards neither of them spoke. There was nothing to say.

Outside in the lane there was the sound of approaching sirens, the screech of metal being cut, vehicles coming and going all the time. Holly had no idea how long it went on, only that the shadows of the latticed windows on the wall were elongated and bathed in a rosy hue when at last Doctor Williamson called. Nearing retirement, Williamson was stout, with a kindly smile; abrupt if he lost patience with you. He looked tired, his greying hair was ruffled, and there was no sign of his jacket – just trousers and braces failing to hide his protruding stomach.

He nodded, smiled and went to the sink to wash his hands. Even then it was almost like a social call. He made small talk as he examined Holly, nodded, and opened up his black bag. 'Nothing wrong with you that a good night's sleep and a couple of these won't put right.' He shook some pink tablets out of a bottle and handed them to Mike. 'And keep her off the whisky for twenty-four hours, old chap. Booze and these don't mix.'

Both men laughed, and Holly found herself laughing with them. That was what Williamson was like: practical, but knew how to get his patients to respond. She felt better already, and the pills had not yet had time to get into her system.

After the doctor had gone, Mike deliberated whether or not to put Holly to bed. It might be easier now before she fell asleep. Before he made his decision there was a knock on the door.

'Good evening, sir, I'm Detective Sergeant Lewis.' The tall detective was unaccompanied. He had parked his unmarked van at the top of the drive. 'Would it be convenient to have a word with you?'

'Can we talk out here?' Mike stepped out on to the patio and pulled the door shut behind him. 'My wife's under sedation, you see. She found the . . . the head!'

'I'm sorry.' The sympathy was routine, like telling a wife her husband has been killed in an accident. The policeman had just completed that duty, and left Mrs Cole in the care of her doctor. A lot of people were under sedation after road accidents. 'You've been having a rough time of it.'

'My wife has. I've been away in London. What's going on, Sergeant?'

'Just another road accident. Our chaps haven't reached their conclusions yet, but it seems that the Land Rover pulled out in front of the cement-mixer. The lorry driver was killed also.'

'And what about this well?' Mike gestured towards the borehole with its propped-up cover and blue pipe leading to the shrubbery. He heard water gushing out into the field beyond. Whatever else had happened, the well was still pumping.

'The *well*, sir?' He raised his eyebrows in astonishment.

'That's what's causing all these deaths, one way or another. What about that . . . that *disease* which the workmen had?'

The detective regarded him thoughtfully before replying. 'The laboratories aren't sure yet, so I can't go into details. I'm sure you'll understand. And I hope you'll keep this to yourself, sir. A public announcement will be made shortly, but we have to be absolutely certain of our facts. Yes, those two fellows *had* got . . . a disease. What it is exactly, the experts aren't sure, but it's something that died out two centuries ago, just as smallpox is now extinct.'

'A . . . *plague*?' Mike felt his mouth go dry, and licked his lips.

'I suppose you could call it that. We had to know some of the facts in case there was a necessity to . . . isolate Garth village. But I can assure you of one thing, sir, if it makes you feel any easier . . . *this virus, and we don't know what it is, cannot be caught by drinking water. It's contagious, which means you have to come into contact with a carrier in order to get it. That much they do know.* It's not like Aids, where you can get it from contaminated blood or the like. Rest assured, sir, polluted your water supply may be, but you won't catch this from it, I'm convinced of that. We checked specially because the victims had been in contact with a polluted well.'

Mike caught his breath and fear knotted his inside. Even if their water did not carry this unknown plague, then both he and Holly had been in contact with Eaton and Fitzpatrick. 'And this latest workman who died, had he got it?' Mike watched the policeman for a reaction to his direct question.

'We're awaiting the post mortem. As you know, there . . . wasn't much left of Cole.' *Just his head, guillotined by the windscreen.* 'It's probably come from some contaminated food in the first place, a freak outbreak. But that's only my personal opinion, you understand.'

'So what do we do in the meantime, Sergeant?'

'Nothing.' The policeman smiled faintly as though to reassure himself as well as Mike Mannion. 'There's no point in isolating the village – these men came from outside. Catching or not, it would be like shutting the door after the horse had bolted. But I'd advise you to contact your doctor if you feel unwell in any way. I'm sorry, I can't tell you more.'

Mike went back indoors. Surprisingly, Holly was still awake. She seemed relaxed and the shock was gone. It was the sedatives, of course.

'What did he want?' She seemed rational, almost normal.

He almost replied 'nothing', but knew she would not be fooled. 'He says that the men died of a plague that hasn't been heard of for two hundred years, and that in no way can the disease be caught from drinking polluted water.'

'Rubbish!'

'Well, we can easily prove or disprove that, Holly.'

'How?' She was sitting up now.

'The well has been flushed out with chlorine, which should kill any germs still in it. We'll get it tested again. If it's pure this time, then we're all right. If not, then I'm going over Kemp's head. I'll write to our MP and demand an investigation. Even though the chlorine might have killed the deadly bugs and it's too late to change what has already happened. An ancient plague unleashed on Britain!' He tried to make a joke of it but his words had a sinister ring to them.

Holly shifted her position and winced. She hadn't made it to town to buy that homeopathic remedy. She turned on to her side.

'What's the matter, Holly?' There was concern on his bearded features.

'That blind boil I get from time to time in an embarrassing place.' She could laugh now that her weight was no longer on it. 'It's coming again, but I'm not going to have it lanced this time. First thing tomorrow I'm going into town for some hepar sulph.'

'Sounds like a witchdoctor's cure.' He regretted his sarcasm immediately.

'It's a homeopathic remedy, and I'll see to it myself,' she retorted. She leaned back, closed her eyes and succumbed to thinking about Nick Paton again. Maybe she would pay him a call on the way back.

Holly had been to town, purchased her tablets and swallowed a couple in a café with a cup of tea. Then she was unable to resist a circuitous return which took her along by the plumber's cottage. As she had feared, he was not at home. One was decidedly lucky to find Nick there before eleven at night. She sighed her disappointment, and the urge which had been dominating her for the past hour subsided. It was just an erotic thought; another time, perhaps.

As she approached Garth Cottage she was surprised to see Bill Kemp's Vauxhall Cavalier parked on the verge. The Environmental Health inspector had wasted no time in returning to test the water. Perhaps there *was* a concern amongst the arrogant, apathetic bureaucracy over the borehole, after all. It was somehow frightening.

'I'll get this tested right away.' Kemp was just leaving, and he touched his cap in an old-fashioned gesture of courtesy to Holly. 'With luck, I'll be able to phone you in the morning. I must say, that awful smell isn't hanging about now. Maybe we've cracked it at last!'

'*The smell isn't around because whatever was down*

there has finally escaped,' Holly muttered as she watched the water inspector stride back to his car.

'Whatever are you talking about?' Mike was abrupt, angry. 'I think you're letting your imagination run away with you. Okay, there might have been some awful disease down there, but there couldn't possibly have been anything more than that.' He looked at her carefully, wondering if he should give Doctor Williamson a call.

'It was just a thought, that's all.' She turned away. She was still walking awkwardly, with a kind of shuffle which she tried to disguise. 'I suppose we may as well try and get back to normal.'

'All right,' he called after her, 'we'll do just that. I'm going to try and get some painting done. You go and rest that sweet little bum of yours.'

She said something beneath her breath but he did not catch it.

It was towards late afternoon on the following day when the telephone rang. Holly had been dozing on the sofa in the kitchen but she responded instantly. She leapt up, then cursed because the boil tweaked her; the hepar sulph was certainly taking its time.

'Hello.' She knew it was Bill Kemp before he spoke.

'At last I've got some good news for you, Mrs Mannion.' He sounded euphoric. 'Your water is pure!'

She nearly giggled in her ecstasy, but Kemp wasn't the type to appreciate those kind of jokes. 'Oh, that's absolutely marvellous,' she answered.

'I'll be confirming it in writing and enclosing a photostat of the laboratory's report.' He was the classic formal civil servant again. He was not obliged to notify them by telephone – his superiors might frown if they knew. He had had no business to show that glimmer of humanity amid the grey background of officialdom. Now he wanted to forget it because he needed the extra money which the job paid.

'Well, that's a relief.' Mike poured boiling water on to

a tea bag, then transferred the steaming spout of the kettle to the mug containing some strange herbal beverage which his wife seemed to enjoy. 'No more time-wasting journeys to the garage to fetch water. Now we can put Garth Cottage on the market!'

'If you're really determined to, then go ahead.' There was resentment in her tone.

'I am!' He was adamant. 'And after all you've been through I should think you would be, too. We can't stay here. At least, I can't.'

'Please yourself.' She stirred her chamomile tea. 'But I think you should phone Frank Bennion and let him know that the water's okay.'

'Tomorrow,' he smiled, 'or perhaps the day after. The bugger will be round five minutes after I've phoned to collect his money. In this hard, realistic economic world, my dear, you learn to hang on to your money for as long as ever you can. Let's make sure there are no more snags before we pay up, or we might not get them rectified quite so readily.'

Holly tossed in an uneasy slumber. Figments of dreams came and went. Some were frightening, but they were gone before she was really afraid. Others were erotic, leaving her in a state of frustration. She was dimly conscious throughout that the base of her spine was smarting, and it hurt if she rolled over on to her back.

The workmen were drilling again. Not Eaton, nor Fitzpatrick; she looked fearfully for them but they were thankfully nowhere to be seen. Strangers, men with caps pulled down so that their faces were hidden in shadow, were boring deep – in a new place this time. She stood watching them through the window, and wondered why they were so close to the cottage. Might their boring disturb the foundations? Why didn't Mike go out and stop them? Why didn't she? Because in dreams you never achieved what you wanted to.

That foul sludge was spurting high into the air,

spraying the surrounding ground with a thick, treacly layer. It didn't appear to be oozing away, following the slope of the land this time, just lying there – stinking! *Oh, Christ, that bloody stench again!* She covered her face with her hands, pinched her nose and tried to hold her breath, but it made no difference. She still smelled the choking putrescence. Gasping for air, she could only draw that odour of rotting flesh down into her lungs. Retching, she thought she might vomit. *For Christ's sake, go out there and tell them to stop!*

The well shaft was wider this time, much wider: a gaping hole, roughly circular, surely several feet in diameter. Just looking at it gave her a sensation of giddiness, and a wave of vertigo forced her to hold on to the windowsill and leave her nostrils unprotected from the stench. The rig was tilted, the ground beneath it was beginning to crack. God, were they blind out there? couldn't they see what was happening?

Then she felt the tremors as the caked surface split. Huge cracks suddenly appeared, and the rig was now wedged across one of them. It was still widening; she felt the cottage shudder, and started to scream for Mike.

Now he was holding her, clutching her to him, and she cried her relief aloud even though the boil on her bottom was agonizing.

'Holly!' She heard his voice, tinged with fear, felt his strong arm crushing her, not just to protect her but because he was afraid also. 'Holly, what's happening?'

'The ground's opening up!' she shouted. 'The cottage will collapse. We'll be buried. . . .'

And suddenly it was no longer a crazy, fragmented dream. It was reality!

She wasn't standing at the window watching the men drill another well; she was in bed with Mike. *But the floorboards were heaving up, furniture was rattling, the whole house was vibrating!*

'Mike . . . what's happening?' She clung to him, buried her face in his hairy torso. But even that could not shut out the vile smell; *that was real too. She tasted it, felt how it seared nostrils and throat, trying to suffocate her with its vileness.*

Then, as suddenly as the disturbance had begun, it subsided. The floor quivered, then became still; the trembling of walls and ceilings ceased. It was quiet – so quiet, she almost believed that it had been a dream. Except for the stench that still lingered, until finally that, too, was gone.

'It was an earthquake.' His voice was unsteady. 'They get them occasionally in this part of the country. I remember reading about a fairly bad one they had around Newtown some years ago. But it's finished now, and let's hope that's the end of it. I expect we'll hear all about it on the radio tomorrow.'

'What time is it, Mike?'

He consulted the luminous dial of his wristwatch. 'Three-thirty. Let's get back to sleep. It's still dark and there's nothing we can do, anyway. At least the cottage is still standing!'

Morning. Mike and Holly had slept late, the slumber of the mentally exhausted which only ended when the rays of the sun found a chink in the curtains and played on their faces, stirring them. Mike looked at his watch again. Nine o'clock. Christ alive!

Holly struggled out of bed with him. Some ornaments on the dressing table had toppled over, a clothes brush shaped like a waddling duck had jettisoned its bristling underbelly on to the floor, and an ashtray loaded with trinkets had spilled its contents.

They dressed quickly but did not pull the curtains open. Downstairs the kitchen was in dissaray: a mug lay shattered on the tiled floor and the fire irons had tipped over and rolled in front of the stove.

Mike was heading for the door, struggling with the key, Holly behind him, her pain temporarily forgotten. Pausing, their gaze met, then dropped. They were scared to go out there, but knew they had to.

They stood on the sunlit patio and stared in disbelief. Holly choked back a scream and clung to her husband. *For down there in the small hollow, where that unsightly concrete structure had poked its deformed head up out of the ground, it was just as it had been in her dream!*

A few fragments of concrete still remained; the rest had doubtless slid down into that wide gaping hole. A roughly circular black abyss yawned with a grotesque mouth. Only the length of blue waste pipe remained, clinging precariously to its fittings as it, too, threatened to slide from view, like the tongue of some fearsome underground reptilian monster in search of human prey. It was utter devastation, and all around was slurry which had been vomited from below, stinking and steaming in the warmth of the morning sun. Driving the two humans back indoors.

Because this time there was no doubt in their minds that whatever had lurked deep in the bowels of the earth and slumbered for centuries awaiting its release, had finally escaped.

13

'It's unbelievable!' Frank Bennion stood on the edge of the crater-like well, peering down nervously into its dark depths. 'Absolutely incredible!'

'What do you think could have caused it?' Mike asked nervously. 'We thought at first it must have been an earthquake . . . but there hasn't been one!' He glanced back towards the cottage and caught a glimpse of Holly's face at the window. The poor girl, he thought, she had been through hell whilst he was away in London. He winced as guilt flooded over him again. Holly was being subjected to sheer terror whilst he was copulating on a whore's bed. But he had to put all that behind him, start afresh.

'The rock fissure has split.' Bennion sounded almost convincing. 'Undoubtedly the drilling was responsible for cracking the rock, and this drought has helped it to expand. But your water's all right now, isn't it?'

'It's fine, at long last.' Mike stiffened. The implication was not lost on him. 'But the job isn't finished – it's one hell of a mess. You can't leave it like this even if there is drinkable water coming out of the taps!'

He risked another look down the hole. The well liner reminded him of a drinking straw leaning in a large empty glass, just propped there, ready for anyone who wanted to suck the dregs up.

'Of course I wouldn't leave it like this!' There was a note of indignation in Bennion's voice. 'It will have to be put right. It's a priority, obviously. I shall have to bring the tack back here and do it myself.'

'Yourself!' Mike could not imagine Bennion in any other role than that of the boss, the country gentleman.

'I don't have a workforce any longer.' There was a touch of bitterness in his voice, and his anger was reflected in the way he kicked a loose piece of shale and sent it spinning down into the shaft. It was some time before they heard a faint splash. 'Three dead, and when I paid the wages last night my other two men asked for their cards. They've been talking amongst themselves, reckon there's a hoodoo on the firm. Stupid bastards! The final straw was Cole – the fool pulled right out in front of that cement-mixer without looking. I shouldn't've trusted him on the job on his own. The fellow was a complete dolt, no more than a mindless labourer. Still, the fact remains that I don't have anybody working for me, and until I can employ more men I've got to go out and do the jobs myself. Still, I did it single-handed in the beginning, and I'm as fit now as I was then. You can expect me at nine in the morning.'

There was both pride and anger in Frank Bennion's upright figure as he stalked back to where the BMW was parked in the entrance to the drive, where the tilted gatepost was a stark reminder of the most recent horror.

'The old boy's going to finish the job himself.' Mike left the kitchen door open; that awful smell had evaporated at last. 'He's a stubborn bugger. Either that or he's just plain greedy and wants my cheque at the earliest possible moment. Well, if he wants to give himself a heart attack struggling with heavy machinery, that's up to him. He needn't look to me to be his fetch and carry boy. I've got too much work to do.'

'I suppose it's all going to start again.' Holly was exceptionally pale today, eyes black-ringed as though she had not slept the previous night. 'The garden will be knee-deep in that dreadful sludge and the place will stink. . . .' She broke off, on the verge of hysteria.

'Look, you ought to go away for a few days.' He regarded her with an expression of concern. 'And when you come back it will all be finished. And the moment that mess is cleared up I'm putting this place up for sale, and no arguments.'

'I don't *want* to go away!' It was almost a shriek. 'I won't leave here until Garth Cottage is sold!'

'All right, have it your own way.' He checked his rising anger. 'If I hadn't got so much work on we'd both go away. But I can't afford to lose many more days. I'm being pushed for the landscapes and I've also got to deliver the first book cover at the end of this month. In fact, I couldn't give a toss what happens out there, to be perfectly candid. If bloody Bennion is writhing on the ground with a hernia, he can stop there – and it's no good shouting for me!' He stalked off, slamming the door behind him.

Only then did Holly get up, and drag herself in a slow, painful shuffle across to the sink. She reached down for the small phial, shook two tablets into the palm of her hand and popped them into her mouth. She picked up a glass and was about to hold it under the tap when realization dawned upon her; instead, she eased her way to the refrigerator, pulled out a half-full carton of fruit juice. No way was she ever going to drink any water that had come from down *there*. Bathing in it was bad enough!

The boil on her tail was not improved – if anything it was worse. She had looked at it again with the help of two mirrors this morning and it was now much bigger, starting to form a head. She tried not to think of Jim Fitzpatrick and those awful weeping ulcers on his mouth. If her boil was no better by tomorrow then she would go and see Doctor Williamson. She shuddered at the prospect of having it lanced but she couldn't go on much longer like this.

In spite of her perpetual discomfort, the urge was upon her again. She was tempted to go upstairs and lie on the bed. No, that would not solve anything; what she had in mind would only increase her craving for Nick Paton. Neither was it any good driving over to his place because he would not be there. She had a feeling of sheer frustration. She could not even finish off the decorating in the lounge, in her state. But it would have to be done before they put the cottage on the market. A couple of days and she might feel better, she consoled herself. She went back to the sofa, slid on to it, made sure that her posterior did not come into contact with any part of it, and lay on her side, staring at the wall.

Mike had been with another woman. She knew that just as surely as if he had admitted it. Only a woman could tell – that intuition again; he was knotted up with guilt. Don't be a bloody hypocrite, she told herself, and laughed out loud. Tit for tat, Holly, my girl, because whilst he's been away you've been having your arse shagged off.

It was going to be a long day and she was already dreading the thought of the morrow when Frank Bennion returned to fill that hole in. With fear, she remembered the way the whole house had shook and shuddered in the night. Just as though some long buried monster which had slumbered a hundred and thirty feet below ground had suddenly awoken and clawed its way to freedom. Awful as that nameless stinking horror had been below ground, the thought of it on the loose was a thousand times worse. What in the name of God could have been interred down there for two centuries that was now spreading this terrible plague?

Frank Bennion arrived at eight-thirty. No longer was he the dapper overseer in smart clothes and green wellington boots; instead he wore a suit of overalls, but had not forsaken his tie. A cap replaced the usual floppy country-style hat, and his hands were encased in thick rubber gloves. The job would be a filthy one, but he obviously intended to keep as clean as possible.

With deft skill he used an ancient Series I Land Rover to tow the heavy rig down to the scene of devastation, the old vehicle labouring under the strain, belching out thick clouds from its rusted upright exhaust. Somehow he got the drill across the open shaft, its wheels resting precariously on the brink. He got out and began busying himself with spanners, his every move positive. Obviously, the watching Holly thought, it had been no idle boast about completing the task himself.

She closed the door and windows in anticipation of that nauseating stench of pumped-up sludge, but decided against closing the curtains. Darkness was not something she relished. She heard the compressor start up with a deafening roar, and eased her way back across the room to the sofa, again positioning herself delicately on her side. Jesus, she was going to have to see the doctor – that was becoming more inevitable by the hour. Evening surgery possibly, and Bennion could move his compressor truck out of the gateway so that she could get the car out.

Mike tried to ignore the din outside. Previously he had

surrendered to it. The excuse to leave had been too readily available in a trip to London; otherwise he would have stuck it out, just as he meant to do now. The studio floor was vibrating, which in turn had his easel quivering. With grim determination he continued to paint, needing every vestige of patience and concentration he could muster.

By eleven o'clock the need for a cup of strong coffee was paramount. He paused, stood back to survey his work and realized how a council roadman operating a pneumatic drill must feel – every nerve in his body was trembling. Only then was he aware of a sensation of discomfort that seemed to be centred upon his navel. He touched it through his shirt, and almost cried out aloud. Bloody hell, it was as if he had a sharp splinter embedded in the flesh of his stomach.

He pulled up his shirt, bent forward to see where the soreness was coming from and stared in horror at what he saw. A swelling approximately the size of a pea protruded from his stomach and seemed to fill his navel. Bloated, a pinpoint of a head filled with matter, it was begging to be squeezed. He touched it gently, then whipped his finger away. Blazes, it was painful!

Now where the devil had he caught that? From a poxy whore! No, it couldn't be. Frightened now, he almost dropped his trousers to check down there again. More likely from Holly, he decided; and that appeased his conscience. Boils were contagious, he seemed to remember reading somewhere. Holly had been lying on her side, facing away from him, in bed last night. They were both naked, and at some time during the nocturnal hours she had rubbed up against him and transferred the germs. So now they both had boils. He tucked his shirt back into his trousers and went through to the kitchen. The soreness didn't seem so bad now.

At first he thought Holly was asleep, but then her tired, distraught eyes flickered open and focused upon him with an expression of near hostility. She hated him for wanting to sell up, he decided. Stupid girl!

'Coffee?' He moved to the stove, where steam was puffing out of the kettle and rattling the lid, except that it was impossible to hear it above the roar of the compressor and the rig outside.

She nodded unenthusiastically. 'All right.'

'By the way.' He put her mug down on the small table by the sofa. 'I think I've caught your complaint.'

'Oh?'

'A boil.'

'Might I ask *where*?' It was an oblique accusation. You have been with a prostitute, she thought, and you're trying to blame it on me. I've only been with Nick, and he's guaranteed clean.

Their gaze met and wavered. He said. 'It's on my *navel*!'

'Oh, I see.'

'Is that remedy you went to town for any good?'

'No.'

'Oh, I see.'

An awkward silence ensued. Mike stood there, angry with her, childishly seeking some kind of revenge for her indifference towards him. He found it. He tugged his shirt up out of his waistband and afforded her a full view of his stomach. Look at *that*, then, he thought.

She stared, and her expression changed to one of horror and revulsion. She pressed herself back into the sofa as though trying to shy away from him. Compelled to look, her eyes focused on that red swelling with its matter-filled head, an evil eye that watched her. 'Oh, my God!'

Her tone frightened him, sobered his petty anger. He had not seen her boil and presumed it to be the same. 'Well, it's like yours . . . isn't it?'

'Not . . . quite,' she whispered. Her head was throbbing now – it was probably because of all the noise. 'Mike, I think we both ought to go and see Doctor Williamson. There's a surgery at six every evening. *Tonight.*'

Her words had a chilling ring to them and he slopped some coffee on to the floor. His mouth was dry, and when he spoke his voice sounded far away, frightened. 'It's . . . it's not one of . . . *those* . . . is it?'

'I . . . don't . . . know.' She was pale and trembling, a pathetic figure hunched up on the settee.

'Oh, God above!'

'Mike, I said I don't *know*. I honestly don't. Maybe it's just an ordinary boil. Navels are a favourite place to get them. A blackhead gone septic, that's all it is. Let's face it, we haven't had many baths for weeks, either of us, just strip washes in water brought up from the garage, used sparingly because we couldn't afford to waste it. It's probably that.'

Probably. He felt a little easier, though. If it hadn't been for recent events he would most likely have just bathed it with TCP and kept an eye on it. All the same, they should see a doctor. He thought about phoning Williamson but decided against it. That would provoke the old man's caustic tongue.

He said in a quavering voice, 'All right, we'll both go down to the surgery tonight.' He sat down on a chair and sipped his drink. The urge to return to the studio was gone. If he managed to do any work then it would not be his best; he would, in all probability, scrap it tomorrow and start from scratch. Sitting there, barely aware of the roar of the machinery outside, he stared at the floor like a man who feared the worst and was waiting to have it confirmed.

Two o'clock. For the first time he was aware that they had sat here for three hours, neither talking nor looking at each other. They would have eaten by now if they were hungry; food was furthest from their minds. Now Holly was speaking, her words penetrating his numbed brain.

'Mike, *I can smell that stench again*!'

He looked up, then smelled it, a wafting rather than the overpowering, stifling, suffocating smell. Enough to make him catch his breath, then it was gone.

'It's bound to smell.' Now it was his turn to be reassuring. 'Bennion's drilling up all that foul muck again. I expect the garden's waist-deep in it.'

'I'm surprised he hasn't knocked off for his lunch.' Holly glanced in the direction of the window. 'Come to think of it, he didn't stop for elevenses, either. At least, he didn't switch the machinery off and he surely would have done if he wasn't using it.'

'Probably knackering himself in order to finish the job so he can get his money.' Mike stood up, but felt slightly weak. 'I suppose I'd better have a look how he's getting on, see how much longer he's likely to be here.' He walked towards the door, gasping under his breath as his belt caught the boil.

He stopped, with the door half-open, and almost slammed it shut again in the hope that what he saw outside was some kind of macabre mirage brought on by this freak heatwave. He stood there, unable to speak, powerless to move. His tortured mind refused to accept what his eyes saw.

'Mike, what is it?'

He heard Holly easing herself off the sofa to join him. He would have stopped her if he could, or else slammed the door shut so that she might be spared the scene out there. But by the time he could move his limbs again it was too late. She had seen it, and was clinging to him, almost fainting.

'*Oh, my God, Mike! It's got him, too!*'

As he had surmised, the garden area was thick with foul sludge which the rig had pumped up out of that bizarre hole in the ground, gallons of it steaming and stinking, and drying in the hot sunshine. That in itself was bad enough, the arcing fountain of slurry hitting the trees, then dripping off them, the machinery grinding and throbbing, bent on desecration of Nature's beauty. Until you saw the still form lying close to the rig, those blue overalls now a muddy greyish brown, the soft hat gone, probably swept away on the slow-moving tide of filth.

One arm lay crumpled beneath the body, the other was outstretched, forefinger pointing towards the mouth of the well.

There was no doubt in Mike's mind that it was Frank Bennion lying there, even though the features were virtually unrecognizable – muddied, the nostrils blocked as if with stinking mucus, mouth agape as though death had struck even as the warning was being shouted and it was now mutely screaming, '*It came up out of there*!'

14

Doctor Williamson's surgery was situated in a brick-built extension to his country mansion on the outskirts of Canon Pine, a village about two miles from Garth. The GP had a wide area to cover. His furthest patients were ten or twelve miles away, and he had become a kind of legend during the twenty or so years since he had taken over the practice after Doctor Andrews' death.

A man who commanded respect, he often advised on matters other than medical ones, and among the farming community his wisdom was held in awe; it would be a devastating blow to the community when eventually he decided to retire. There were rumours that he was on the verge of seeking a more relaxed way of life during his declining years, but he refuted them. A year ago he had taken on a younger partner, Doctor Bell, and there was talk that the older man was about to hand over the reins. But, in reality, Williamson just needed somebody to share the increasing workload, the difficult journeys to an emergency in the Range Rover during bad weather. Sadly, during surgeries, the majority of patients stubbornly demanded to see only Williamson, whilst Bell waited in vain in his empty consulting room. Only recently had they, rather reluctantly, accepted the junior partner. That was country life – nothing must change.

Mike parked in the road outside the doctor's house. It was hot, probably ninety in the shade, he reckoned. He walked around to the other side of the car, opened the door and helped Holly to ease herself painfully out of the passenger seat, wincing at her gasp of pain beneath her breath. His own ulcer was just as sore, but fortunately he was not compelled to sit upon it. The two of them stood there, holding on to each other, scared to go in through the wrought-iron-gates, afraid of the diagnosis. Not talking, they inwardly wished they had not come, that they had given their ailments another day in the hope that they might heal themselves. In hope and fear they eased their way down the gravel drive with dense laurels on either side, an untidy sprinkling of dead brown leaves crackling beneath their shuffling feet. Today was what Doctor Williamson termed 'country surgery', an additional consultation session held from half-past twelve to four, primarily to encourage outlying patients to make the journey in rather than ringing for a visit. It saved time and petrol, and conserved an ageing man's energy; the patients saw it as yet another demonstration of their revered doctor's unselfishness.

The reception area was deserted. There was an empty window with some pigeonholes behind it containing prescriptions to be collected and a hand bell on the sill to summon attention.

'Ah, good afternoon.' A small rotund woman appeared from an adjoining doorway and gave a welcoming smile, her grey hair neatly fastened up on the top of her head in a bun. Mike presumed she was the doctor's wife acting as receptionist. 'Can I help you?'

'Thanks.' *God I wish you could.* 'Mannion's the name, Mike and Holly, Garth Cottage. We'd like to see Doctor Williamson.'

'I'm sorry' – they got the impression that her apology

was sincere – 'but Doctor Williamson's not here this afternoon, he's been called away urgently. Would you like to see Doctor Bell?'

Mike hesitated, then glanced at Holly. It was Williamson they wanted; he *might* just understand. They could come back this evening. Or tomorrow morning. Or tomorrow evening. In the meantime, the ulcers might have burst, healed. No, they wouldn't; he knew they would just grow bigger and. . . . 'All right, we'll see Doctor Bell.' His tone was reluctant.

'Go through to the waiting room, please. He won't keep you many minutes.'

There was no one in the large waiting room, just a table piled with well-thumbed magazines in the middle and chairs lining the walls. Neither Holly nor Mike picked up a glossy publication, and they were grateful that there was nobody else to witness their anguish.

'This is the third time I've had this blind boil. Or is it the fourth?' She told her husband what her own ears wanted to hear, forcing herself to believe it and wanting him to, also. 'I suppose I'm stuck with it, and it'll happen every few years.'

'I must have caught mine from you. Not that I'm blaming you.' Finding reasons, excuses – anything as long as it wasn't to do with the borehole, he thought.

A buzzer sounded. Mike and Holly looked at each other. Who was going first, or should they go in together? A few moments of hesitation and then they began another shuffle across the slippery polished linoleum.

Doctor Bell was in his early forties, with wavy dark hair and a boyish smile. He was still struggling to win the confidence of the locals; he liked it when the 'old man' was out because they didn't have a choice, which gave him the chance to win them over. With his tweed jacket and grey flannels, he hoped he gave a rural impression; it wasn't easy when you had moved from London. 'Now, what's the problem?' He pressed the tips of his fingers together, sensing an embarrassment which embarrassed him, too.

'We've . . . er, we've both got . . . boils,' Mike stammered, pulling up his shirt and watching for a reaction on the doctor's face, but there was none, just a leaning forward. 'My wife's is in . . . a rather . . . more tender place.'

'I see.' Bell came round the desk, scrutinized the infected navel, touched it gently and heard his patient grunt and stiffen. 'Nasty, but common enough. I think I'll have to lance it, but first I'm going to give you a course of antibiotics to see if that will do the trick. Looks to me as if you've been rubbing on something.'

Mike closed his eyes to hide the guilt in them. That bloody whore, that was where it had come from. And he'd passed it on to Holly. A kind of VD of the navel, but it spread where it touched.

Bell was back at his desk scribbling something on an index file, then writing out a prescription. 'I'd better have a look at yours just to see that it's the same as your husband's, Mrs Mannion.'

Mike did not want to look and wished that Doctor Bell had asked him to step outside. But it was impossible not to peer past the doctor when he leaned over Holly as she lay on the examination couch with her denim shorts around her ankles. Mike heard her bite back a cry of pain and saw the ugly swelling, the head threatening to burst, full of vile matter.

'Hmm.' The doctor straightened up and Mike jerked back, trying to create the impression that he was more interested in a hunting scene on the wall. 'Same goes for you, Mrs Mannion. Antibiotics and then, if it doesn't burst by the day after tomorrow, I'll fix it.' He was writing again, ripping another sheet off his pad. 'The chemist in town, Blurton's in the High Street, is open till six. The sooner you start the course, the better.'

'Doctor. . . .' Mike's mouth was dry, his words did not want to come. He felt like a child trying to pluck up the courage to ask an awe-inspiring parent a delicate question. 'Tell me . . . it isn't . . . I mean, it's not one of . . . *them*, is it?'

'Whatever are you talking about, Mr Mannion?' It might just have been genuine bewilderment on Bell's features. He had put his glasses on, seemed suddenly sombre, and was doodling on his jotter.

'The . . . the *disease*,' Mike's head was thrust forward and he felt a sudden desire to scream his worst fears aloud. 'What those two men died of, Bennion's workmen – and now Bennion himself.'

'I've no idea what they died of.' Bell dropped his gaze, then looked up again. 'All I know is that three men died and there is an autopsy taking place. They weren't my patients or Doctor Williamson's. Whatever you're worrying about, forget it. You've both got nasty boils, the common or garden sort. One of you started with one, and in all probability infected the other. Now, does that answer your question, put your mind at rest?'

Mike nodded, not trusting himself to speak immediately. All too pat, he thought, stalling them with drugs and hope to God it clears up. He wanted to believe the doctor. If it wasn't the well then it was that prostitute, and maybe antibiotics would do the trick. 'Thanks, we'll go and get the pills.'

'Fine. If the boils aren't gone in forty-eight hours, come back. If they are . . . give me a ring, will you, please?'

Mike tautened as the room seemed to spin. We're guinea pigs, he thought, the first live ones. The others had died. The doctor was trying drugs, hoping, because he couldn't think of anything else. He was just playing a game, deceiving the patient, because there wasn't anything else to do. The centuries-old plague was beyond the dawn of modern medicine.

'Well, that's that.' Holly was sitting in an uncomfortable kind of twisted position in the passenger seat, two smoky plastic bottles clutched in her sweating hand. 'We don't have any choice, Mike.'

'Bell *says* they're common boils.' He made yet another attempt to console himself and his wife. 'For the moment we've got to go along with that.'

'All right,' she whispered. It was an effort to talk. 'Let's treat them as boils, then. Until we find out otherwise.'

On the familiar stretch of road, Holly found herself tensing, glancing almost furtively along the opposite verge, knowing that there would be a gateway a few yards round the next bend, a view of the renovated cottage which stood at the bottom of the steep drive. It would have a deserted look about it, an emptiness that hurt. She hoped Mike wasn't watching her, that he would not notice her intensity. She was sweating, trembling.

The sudden shock hit her as hard as if she had carelessly changed position and put her weight on that boil. Searing, hurting, she felt a desire to leap from the moving car and rush heedlessly down the drive. Because the cottage wasn't deserted; an Escort van with ladders and drain rods strapped to the roof was parked outside the door. Nick Paton was at home!

She closed her eyes and felt her brain reeling. What the hell was Nick doing at home? He was never home before late evening, often not before the early hours. The urge was almost overpowering. She had to see him, talk to him. Before it was too late.

Back home, it was another slow trip from the car to the cottage, Holly wanted to shake off Mike's supporting arm. Her burning desire almost transcended physical pain. She was trying to walk normally. God it was agony!

They swallowed their pills, drinking orange juice to wash them down because neither of them could face the water out of that hell-hole outside. She leaned up against the fridge and found a comfortable position.

'Will you be all right for a while?' That meant he was going through to the studio to paint. In all probability he would be gone for hours once he got started. She hoped so.

'I feel much better,' she lied, wondering what excuse she could find for going out, and if she was physically capable of taking the car.

'Call me if you need me.' He clinked his glass in the sink. 'I'll have to press on with the work, regardless.'

'You do that.' She managed a smile. The bottom of her spine felt as though it was smouldering like a length of damp kindling which would burst into flames when it dried out. 'I'll be fine.'

'Good.' He was on his way to the door when suddenly he turned to the window and peered out. 'There's a vehicle coming in through the gate. A van. That CID man again, I suppose.' His groan that turned to mild surprise. 'No, it isn't the police. It's the plumber!'

Holly thought for one second that she was going to faint, as from the depths of despair euphoria rose like a phoenix out of the fire. Holding on to the fridge until the feeling passed, she waited until she could trust herself to speak. Then she said, 'You carry on, Mike. I know you've an awful lot of work to catch up on. I'll see to the plumber. Mostly he knows what has to be done, so he'll probably just get on with it and won't need either of us.'

'Good.' Mike smiled and went out. 'See you later.'

Holly was sweating, weak with relief. It was as though Nick had been made aware of her craving for him and had come in answer to a telepathic summons. Her whole body seemed to be on fire, the flames of lust consuming everything within her, even the pain.

She heard the van stop, the engine die and a door slam. She made her way across to the sofa and was oblivious of any discomfort as she stretched herself out on it. Damn you, Mike Mannion, she thought. Why the hell didn't you stop in London out of the way!

Doctor Williamson had not hurried on the steep, twisting journey up through the hills above Garth village. It was hot in the Range Rover, and at one point he pulled in to a wide stony lay-by to look down on the cluster of houses below. It was like a toy farmyard untidily strewn by a careless child, a magical haphazardness about it which was absent in modern-day planning, where everything had to be symmetric. Garth had grown up like the gorse and bracken on the slopes above it, a process that had taken centuries; a dwelling was needed so it was built, out of stone from the quarry and timber beams from the forest, hewn by hand. It was an ancient habitation, populated by peasants who lived a simple life and left no written records. He could only guess at their life style. They grew their simple food, reared their animals for meat, hunted deer in the hills. And now . . . he was as guilty as any of these so-called outsiders; even from here he could make out his own house back at Canon Pine, its new extension standing out stark and ugly against the old brickwork. He needed a place in which to treat the sick, but it could have been built of stone and timber, not unsightly glaring red mass-manufactured brickwork that would crumble to dust long before the local stone of the big house which it adulterated.

He screwed up his eyes against the glare of the afternoon sun, ignoring the black flies which swarmed and settled on him. The smell of the hills was sweet, heady; unchanged since time immemorial. Yet there was *something* here, something even he could not understand. He sensed it in the atmosphere and felt a fear of the unknown. It emanated from the village, spread out like an invisible cloud and ate into him. The tension would not go away, and his mounting uneasiness meant that he did not sleep easily, and woke up and stared into the darkness, sensing a presence. But when he switched the light on there was nothing there. Childish fears, he tried to convince himself unsuccessfully. Those deaths – the workman, Fitzpatrick, was the only one he had seen for himself. Williamson had found himself shying away from the corpse, and he had seen death in many terrible forms throughout his life: cancers that had rendered their victims virtually skeletal, road accidents where the dead were unrecognizable mulches. But that one . . . he could see it even now, *sores that pulsed even after life had deserted the wretched body, spreading and feeding on the dead flesh with revolting rapidity and cancerous lust.*

Today he was on his way to witness a death, but this

time it would be natural, peaceful, a termination of a long and healthy life. Old Josh Owen was ninety-four, or was it ninety-five? Anyway, a quarter of a century bonus on his allotted lifespan. He might have made the century – his father had, just. But that was before the doctor came to Canon Pine.

Owen was a typical hill man, a smallholder who had farmed his fifty acres the way his father and grandfather and the rest of his line had before him, resisting change; no machinery, no running water or electricity. Water came from the brook in the dingle, warmth from the kindling in the forest. He ate simple food: milk from the house cow to drink and make cheese, rabbits snared in the heather. He went abroad in all weathers, drying off in front of the fire, going to bed when it was dark and getting up at first light. A *natural* way of life, Williamson thought, which was why he had outlived his neighbours who had succumbed to the march of civilization. But now Owen's time was nigh, and the doctor would be with him at the end; there was no point in trying to fight the inevitable, the old man would not thank him for it. Maybe Owen was already dead. Williamson hoped so, which was why he was not hurrying, idling here and trying to admire the view, watching the graceful glide of a buzzard above the valley as it floated on its ragged, moth-like wings, hunting its prey. Like himself, it was waiting for death.

Josh Owen was still alive. Williamson forced the warped door open, squeezed through into the small, sparsely furnished room and saw the old farmer sitting up on the couch which had served him for a bed since boyhood. Grimed sheets matched his weatherbeaten countenance and he was still wearing a ragged cap because he refused to concede that he was bald. Toothless, pouting his hardened gums, blowing out his cheeks as he breathed with difficulty, he smiled in his own inimitable shrunken way, knowing that he was going to die and welcoming the end because there was nothing left to live for now that he was confined indoors.

The doctor did not enquire after his health. Both of them were only too well aware of the situation, and up in the hills you did not waste time with trivialities. Nod and answering nod, then Williamson pulled up a stool and lowered his bulk on to it. The farmer was breathing heavily; the end would not be long and the doctor would sit it out with his patient. The old eyes closed, the head sank a little. Not long now. Outside that buzzard was mewing its plaintive hunting cry directly over the tumble-down dwelling as though even it scented death.

Then Josh Owen opened his eyes, and Williamson saw that they were bright and clear, alert and understanding. Another puff of the hollowed cheeks and the toothless lips began to move. When Owen finally spoke there was no slurring of his voice, just a matter-of-fact tone. His body was tense, upright, fighting off death because he had something to say and his Maker would not mind waiting another few minutes.

'Listen, doc, there's bad things happenin' down Garth, ain't there?'

'Yes.' Williamson felt that this gloomy abode had suddenly gone chilly. There was no point in denying what Owen said; maybe he sensed it, too, even up here, a thousand feet or more above Garth. The evil, whatever it was, knew no boundaries.

'There's death down there,' those cracked lips rasped, dribbling a string of spittle. 'And there'll be more afore it's done, you mark my words. I thank God that I'll be gone soon.'

The doctor shuddered. Maybe somebody had been up here talking to Josh Owen. He could think of no other explanation. But these certainly were not the ramblings of a man who had come to the end of his time. Williamson nodded but didn't speak. If the farmer wanted to say any more, he would.

'Listen.' There was an urgency about Owen now. He glanced towards the window, for the sun was his only guide to the passing of time. 'There's somethin' I have to tell you, doc, and may the Good Lord grant me time enough to say it.' His lungs wheezed and he coughed up a blob of phlegm.

'Go on.' Williamson leaned forward. 'I'm listening.'

'I'm only a-tellin' you what my father and 'is father told me once, for what it's worth, the legend of Garth, handed down by word of mouth over the centuries. I only knows what was passed on, and as I've no children to tell it to, I may as well tell you, otherwise it'll be lost for all time. You see' – he paused and checked the sun again – 'sometime, I dunno how long ago, there was a feller lived in Garth, a big strong feller, who got a notion to travel to the city and see what 'e was missing. What 'e found there, nobody knows, except 'e got into the devil's clutches for sure, and when 'e came back to Garth 'e was dyin' from some terrible plague, a livin', festerin' thing 'e was!'

Williamson found himself glancing into the shadowy corners of the room, his earlier unease mounting. A legend, perhaps, embellished over the years, but he saw again in his mind Jim Fitzpatrick's corpse with those pulsing sores feeding on it. He shivered uncontrollably.

'This feller, I don't recall bein' told 'is name, returned and crawled into a cowshed to die. Folks would've left 'im there, maybe burned it down and 'is body with it, except the Witchfinder arrived and called for them to drag 'im out. They hanged 'im, this chap with the plague, but the Witchfinder told them not to gibbet 'im because the plague was a terrible one. They were ordered to bury 'im as deep as they could dig, and the story goes that they dug for two whole days until they had a grave as deep as a well. Then they dropped 'im in and filled in the shaft. Whether any of 'em caught this plague my father didn't say, only that the corpse was crawlin' with livin' ulcers that fed on the flesh until all that was left to bury was a mass o' pulsin' growths!'

'My God!' Doctor Williamson felt slightly sick. It couldn't be, it was medically impossible, it defied all the laws of disease and modern science. *And yet he had witnessed this very same festering death with his own eyes*!

'Did your father say' – the doctor moved across to the window – 'exactly where this grave was situated?'

There was no reply, and when Doctor Williamson turned round he saw that the old shepherd was lying back on the cushion that served as a pillow, those bright eyes closed as if the effort of talking had tired him and he slept.

Only the doctor knew, before he checked the pulse on the leathery wrist, that Josh Owen would never talk again. If the smallholder had known the site of the deep grave, then he had taken his secret with him.

15

Nick Paton stood in the open doorway, squinted and waited for his eyesight to adjust to the gloom after the brilliant sunshine outside. Holly studied him carefully, her initial excitement at his arrival tempered by his haggard, unkempt appearance. His hair was awry, his eyes were hollowed and red-rimmed as though he had not slept. Overworking, she thought. It had caught up with him in the end.

'Hi.' She shifted her position slightly and endured the pain which it brought. 'Fancy seeing you, Nick! I was just thinking about paying you a visit. I saw the van at home when we drove past about an hour ago.'

'Yeah.' He stroked his chin and leaned up against the doorpost. 'From now on I'm working virtually full-time for Bennions. My own customers are screaming blue murder, so I've taken the phone off the hook. Bennion's missus asked me to finish off all the existing wells that are still uncompleted, so as the rig and compressor were here I thought this would be a good place to start.'

'I'm glad.' she smiled. 'By the way, my husband's here. In his studio. Not that he's likely to emerge for the next three hours!' She gave a laugh. 'Are you sure you're okay?'

'I've been feeling a bit off the hooks today.' He moved into the room and stood by the settee. 'I guess I'm doing too much. Christ almighty, what the blazes has been going on here? First the workmen, then another killed out on the road. Now Frank. They reckon it was a heart attack.'

'Do they?' There was relief in her voice.

'Well, he asked for it, trying to do the whole job on his own at his age, all that heavy lifting, plus working himself up into a tizz because he didn't know how to cope.'

Holly wasn't listening. Her entire body seemed on fire, trembling in every nerve, and even the pain was forgotten. Memories of the other night fired her escalating lust as her eyes focused on the lower half of her companion's body. Nick wasn't wearing his overalls today, probably because it was too damned hot, just a pair of thin, worn jeans. Her fingers edged outwards and began to stroke him from the knee upwards. She felt him trembling in time with herself. Oh, God, I don't care if Mike is home, she thought. I can't stop myself!

'Hey!' It was a weak protest from the plumber as she ran his zip, delved inside the open vent, found what she was seeking and dragged it out into the open. His knees buckled and found a resting place against herself. With pouted lips, then a flicking tongue, she kissed him, deliriously, holding his legs in case he tried to escape her clutches.

A minute, no more, and she was smiling up at him as she wiped her lips, her body still crazed with desire. But he had backed off and extricated himself from her hold, and her groping fingers met with just an empty space. He was flushed, zipping himself up, avoiding her gaze. 'Nick, I . . . want . . . you.'

'Steady on, your hubby might come in.' He moved away still further. 'Right now I've got to get on with some work. Can't figure out how that well opened up like that, but it's got to be filled in. I reckon the best way is to order a load of ready-mix and concrete it in good and proper.'

'In case there's anything still down there?'

He stared, paling visibly. 'Whatever do you mean?'

'You know as well as I do, Nick, that there was *something* down that hole. It's killed men, and caused them to murder people they loved. Whether it's gone or not, I don't know. I thought perhaps it had, but I'm not so sure now. *The smell, you can always trace it by its vile stench, whatever it is. Oh, Nick, what can it be*?'

He shook his head and seemed reluctant to go outside, glancing through the doorway, hanging back . . . because now he, too, was afraid. 'I . . . don't know. Maybe, like you say, it's gone. But *where*?' He hesitated. Maybe it had been a mistake to come to Garth Cottage in the first place. He should have known better after last time. This girl was a right raver, he realized, a nympho who couldn't get enough. Sex crazy! But she was scared, all right, no mistake about that. And who wouldn't be, after the events of the past few days?

'Nick?'

'Yes?' He didn't look up; her eyes were hypnotic, there was no knowing what she would do to him. And it would be plain crazy with her husband just round the corner in that artist's shed of his.

'I . . . Nick, I want you to . . . *destroy* whatever it is down in the well. *If* it's still down there.'

'*Destroy* it! Are you crazy. How. . . .'

'There is a way, you suggested it yourself. *Ready-mixed concrete, cement the lot up, the liner as well, trap whatever it is down there for good.*'

'Jesus almighty! Mrs Bennion would have my guts for garters. They haven't had a penny on the job so far, and even when they get paid it'll be a loss after all the disasters.'

'I don't care, Nick. Just do as I say, fill it in with concrete!'

'I'll have to get Mrs Bennion's say-so first. I daren't. . . .'

'Sod Mrs bloody Bennion!' Holly had swung her feet to the ground, her eyes were smouldering. '*They* cocked it up, and the customer is pissed off with the whole performance. That's an order. *Fill it in with concrete*!'

'All right.' He was shaken. 'But first I'll have to go and have a look, and see how much cement we're likely to need. But we won't be able to order it till first thing in the morning because the sand and gravel firm close at five-thirty sharp. And even if you order first thing in the morning there's no guarantee that you'll get a delivery the same day. Depends on how many deliveries they've got scheduled.' Stall her, he thought. She's gone plumb crazy, this thing's got to her.

'Go and look, then.' Her voice sounded different, he noticed, rasping as if she had a bad case of tonsilitis or something. 'And when you've done your calculations, come back and let me know. And *I'll* phone for the cement if it makes you feel any easier!'

He went out into the hot sunshine, suddenly glad to be out of the cottage. There was something wrong with Holly Mannion; he glanced back just to make sure that she wasn't following him. All this business had made her flip her lid, he guessed.

Nick found himself approaching the open well shaft with caution. Shitfire, it really looked as if something had clawed its way out of there. Or else somebody had detonated a charge of explosive at the bottom of the well. There were muddy footprints all around, dried hard by the sun, and another indentation that . . . resembled a human shape! He backed away; no, it was probably where one of the coppers had lain to look down into the hole. He told himself that over and over again until he almost believed it. In any case, Bennion had had a heart attack, nothing like . . . Eaton and Fitzpatrick. And Cole had been killed in a road accident – that could happen to anybody. *Get a bloody grip on yourself, Nick Paton.*

He knelt down and steeled himself to peer over the edge. Just blackness, nothing else; he could not see more than a couple of metres or so down. *Use your torch.* I don't want to see, he argued. *You'll have to.* But I can tell her anything I like, and fuck her if there's either too much or not enough ready-mixed. He was curious now; something had caused the well to split open, and he knew that if he found the cause he'd sleep easier in his bed.

He felt in his pocket for the small torch he always carried, but realized it wouldn't be big enough, he'd have to use the large rechargeable one out of the van. He got to his feet and swayed slightly. *Jeez, keep away from that hole!* He wasn't well, he hadn't been feeling right for a day or so now – a sore throat, headache, distorted vision at times. Just over-doing it, he told himself. You'll have to relax a bit more, Nick, my boy.

He went and fetched the torch, taking his time. However strong it was, he realized it wasn't going to shine right down to the bottom. Maybe he should haul the submersible pump up. If Holly really meant what she said there was no point in burying an item of valuable equipment needlessly. Yes, pull it up, he decided. He could always put it back afterwards. But he had to switch it off first. He looked towards the control box on the side of the house. Another delay – maybe he could think up a few more. Or, better still, come up with some good reason that would convince Holly that they could not fill the well in.

There was a sour taste in his mouth. It had been there all day, reminding him of a day-old onion flavour. Onions never had agreed with him, so he never ate any. Which meant it wasn't onions he could taste – he wasn't thinking straight. Maybe tomorrow he would have a day in bed, and lock the doors in case that sex-mad bitch called round.

He flicked the torch on and dropped down on his

hands and knees. He felt dizzy, but if he just slid to the edge, leaned over and shone the beam down a bit . . . what was the point? None, really. He was going through the motions, in case she was watching him through the window. He'd give her some figures and let her sort the mess out.

He could just see over the brink now, a ragged circular shape that cast its own black shadows, cold and forbidding. He remembered seeing on the television a year or so back how a child had fallen down a well and been trapped there for days. Miraculously, the rescue force had got her up alive by digging a parallel shaft to reach her. Ugh! But he knew he had to look. Just a peep. Purely academic.

What was that? He jumped, almost dropping the torch. A noise, like something moving. *Down there!* He was sweating, then shivering; there was a cold blast of air coming up from the borehole, chilling the perspiration on his body. Probably a lump of rock had dislodged and fallen down to the bottom he told himself. He could still hear the sound. *It was as though somebody was breathing heavily down there, wheezing, groaning.*

It was the wind in the shaft, he thought, but knew there wasn't any wind! Well, maybe air was being sucked in somewhere. Or else the pump was making a peculiar noise.

It had stopped now. The deathly stillness had an atmosphere of foreboding about it, as if whatever had made that moaning sound was . . . waiting! Well, shine the bloody torch down there and see, he challenged. You're imagining all sorts of things because you're overtired. And ill.

He had to make a supreme effort, but he poked his head over the hole, held the flashlight downwards and flicked the switch. Instinctively he closed his eyes. If there *was* anything down there, he didn't want to see it!

Then he felt the icy blast, a gust of foul arctic air that came rushing up from below, fastened its freezing dead fingers around his wrist. He cried out, meaning to scream but it came out like a suffocated grunt. He tried to wriggle back from the edge but his limbs would not respond, and he held his breath because of the stench of foul putrefaction. He felt the torch slip from his fingers, as though whatever had hold of his hand had wrested it angrily from him. It hit the side of the shaft and the glass shattered. Then it went on down . . . he found himself counting, the way he had when he was a small boy and his parents had taken him to see the Wishing Well in Tamworth Castle. He'd dropped a pin and counted until he'd heard it go *plop* in the water at the bottom. He couldn't remember how many he had counted to then, but he was up to twenty-two now – and that torch must have weighed five kilos!

He heard it hit something, *but it wasn't water*! There was a kind of sickening squelchy thud as if the heavy object had hit soft matter. His frightened brain conjured up something illogical, something *repulsive*. He didn't know what; he pictured a shape out of a fevered nightmare, bulbous and indefinable, a stinking morass that shifted and oozed like a fat slug on a damp night – evil, cold to the touch.

He lay there, scared to open his eyes, feeling it all around him, its malignant odours trying to choke him. He couldn't breathe. He retched, vomited and tasted bile in his dry mouth. Like in a bad dream, he was unable to move as it stroked him with deathly wet hands and seeped inside his clothing. It was in his lungs, torturing them with its filthy presence, pounding his heart and pulses until surely they could stand no more. And then, suddenly, it was gone.

He still tasted it and smelled it, but his lungs were gasping in fresh warm air, reviving him. The sun was reheating his body until the fevered sweat returned to saturate his grubby shirt. He opened his eyes but turning his head away so that he did not have to look at the well.

Slowly he got back on to his knees, then rested a minute or two before trusting his legs with his full weight. He was shaken, frightened, but physically unhurt. There was a foul coating on his tongue, a taste of bile and decomposition. He began to walk away from the well – would have run if he had been able. Heading towards the van, he wondered if he was capable of driving it; then altered direction towards the cottage.

He had to warn Holly, but perhaps he was too late already. Whatever had arisen from the depths had passed over him, left him and gone elsewhere. *Where?* It was true what Holly Mannion had said; something evil lurked in the borehole, and he had foolishly ridiculed her. He had interfered with it, planned to destroy it, and it had warned him: *I can destroy you just as I destroyed the others, crazed their brains and festered their bodies.*

He staggered up to the kitchen door. It was still open but there was no sign of Holly lying on the settee in a seductive pose, just empty chairs, and the kettle boiling on the stove. Then he saw that the door to the hallway was ajar, creaking on its hinges as though whoever had passed through had been in too much of a hurry to close it after them. *Because they were fleeing from some nameless terror.*

He tried to shout her name but only incoherent sounds came from his lips. Panicking, he wanted to flee this dreadful place, but knew that he could not leave Holly Mannion to the mercy of —

'Nick! Oh, thank God!'

Holly appeared in the doorway and leaned against the lintel for support. Breathless, near to fainting, she too was having difficulty in speaking. 'Oh, Nick . . . I . . . I can't find Mike!'

'Can't . . . find . . . Mike. . . .' He had to repeat her words in an attempt to understand. His thinking was momentarily fogged by fear. Then he began to understand, with a new terror. Not Holly but her husband was missing.

'Nick . . . *do you hear me? Mike is missing. I can't find him anywhere!*'

He nodded, understanding only too well. He recalled how that thing had touched him with its diseased body, its smell; how it could have taken him as it had the others, but had chosen to pass on.

And now Mike Mannion was nowhere to be found.

16

Mike Mannion made a determined effort to concentrate on his work. It wasn't easy. His concentration lapsed and he found his brushwork indecisive. Standing back, he made every effort to admire his artwork and failed miserably. Trying too hard, he thought. Usually he just painted, let the brush take over. But today the tool of his trade was as sluggish as he was.

It was what he termed 'butterfly' painting: dodging from one part of the canvas to another, touching up where it was not necessary and regretting it afterwards. Of course, it was all due to that well outside – how could anybody work after *that*! And overall it was Holly's fault, he decided. It was she who had insisted on moving out to the country, taking on a whole host of unnecessary problems which were costing them a fortune. If they had remained where they were, life would have been a doddle and they would have had ample spare money. Now most of his advance would go on a stinking deep hole that had caused four deaths already. And might be responsible for more!

It was certainly the borehole that had brought about this terror. In the beginning he had scoffed at the suggestion, now he knew. He hoped the plumber wouldn't be able to fix it – that would let them off the hook. No water, no payment, Bennion had said. All right, they had water – but there was a hole which was the equivalent of a mine shaft in the garden, and you didn't pay for botch-ups like that. No way. Getting it filled in might cost a hundred or two, but with Bennion dead nobody was going to press too hard for the money. They'd tidy it up, put Garth Cottage on the market and, who knew, they might even make a small profit! And he was determined their next house was going to be situated in some nice little suburb with all mod cons, water out of the tap provided by the water authority.

Suddenly he was aware of the smell, that now familiar penetrating odour which got you before you realized it. He jerked his head away but there was no escaping the stench. It was thick and strong, a combination of what might waft up out of an open septic tank and a well-rotted compost heap where the odd dead animal had been thrown in for good measure. He turned away and spat on the floor in an attempt to cleanse his mouth. Jesus!

His revulsion turned to fear. *For was not the foul stench a forerunner of that invisible force that brought death and disease?* He backed away, meaning to go through into the house to check that all the windows were closed, but he had barely taken two paces before the pain hit him. Gut-wrenching agony bent him double, making him clutch at his stomach, then snatch his fingers away with a cry of pain and fear. It was as though some sharp instrument was penetrating his abdominal flesh, trying to disembowel him. He fell to his knees and tugged up his shirt to look – and that was the moment he almost fainted.

No, it could not be true! His navel appeared to have swollen to the size of a tennis ball, a fat red object with a stinking slippery surface where the pus had oozed out of the straining head. Thick matter gave off a nauseating smell, and it had already dripped on to his jeans, leaving a yellowish stain where the denim had absorbed it. *And his navel – or was it an ulcer of gigantic proportions? – was swelling even as he watched in horrified revulsion, and might burst at any second!*

His instinct was to grip it, squeeze the poison out, but he dared not touch it. It was hot – he could feel the feverish heat that came from it. *Oh, my God, I have to see a doctor!*

Fighting for logic, he resisted the urge to dash into the kitchen and confront Holly with it. No, she was diseased herself, he realized. That thing on her arse was one of these very same sores! *We're both going to die! Please, God, save us!*

He needed to see Doctor Williamson. The phone was in the kitchen, but so was Holly. A dilemma. He knelt and tried not to look down upon his cancerous stomach; making his decision, he hauled himself back up on to his feet. The car was parked behind the house. If he could still drive, five minutes' motoring would bring him to the surgery at Canon Pine. He went outside, checking that there was nobody about. The plumber was lying down peering into the well; Mike walked swiftly, kept to the browned grass until he reached the car, then he slid in behind the wheel, taking care not to rub himself against it. He pressed the starter and the engine fired; the gears grated once, and then he was moving forward.

Even in his terror he recalled that accident with the Land Rover and the cement-mixer, and checked that the lane was clear of traffic before he pulled out into it. His vision was blurred, so he eased his foot off the throttle and ensured that he kept well to the left, scuffing the verge in places.

His thoughts were as erratic as his driving. That prostitute, what was her name? He couldn't remember, but he saw her now as clearly as he had on that night. A naked bitch, just wanting his money. Hell, if he could be with her again, he'd have his money's worth, no doubt about that! Arousal and anger, a strange combination, transcended the gnawing pain in his navel. There was damp on his trousers again; he found it exciting.

He slowed down when he came to the thirty mph sign, unable to read it but knowing what it was. This was where the straggling village of Canon Pine began. Now where the hell was the doctor's house? He knew it was along here somewhere, a stone-built place with an extension to the west wing. He slowed to a halt, and sat there undecided; maybe it would be easier to find it on foot. Except that this sore festering on his navel was weeping fast now, spewing its pus all down him. Then he heard somebody coming, heard the fast tip-tap of feet before a figure emerged out of the fog that shrouded his vision. A girl! His pulses raced and the agony in his stomach began to recede as more powerful feelings dominated him. A woman, anyway. She was no chicken, attractive and . . . he caught his breath as the shock of recognition sent a wave of dizziness over him. He fought it off, groped for the door handle and depressed it. Jesus Christ almighty, this was becoming crazier by the second! The back of his neck goosepimpled. Here, in Canon Pine – it was unbelievable! For the approaching woman was none other than the whore he had visited in London. And, as if to dispel any doubt he might have had, he could even recall her name now – Joanna!

He slid out of the car and let the door swing shut. She was almost level with him now, walking purposefully along the pavement, her long hair swinging from side to side. Mike's eyes narrowed lustfully as he saw through the flimsy cotton dress, remembering every detail of her passable figure: the artificial tan, the way her nipples stood firm and hard. He was breathing fast. He had not forgotten their last meeting, and his anger was aroused as well as his desire for her body again. This time, sweetheart, he vowed, we're really going to screw!

'Hi, there!' His voice sounded distant, scarcely recognizable as his own. In fact, he wondered if she had heard him, but as she turned into the drive immediately opposite, she stopped. There was an expression of puzzlement on her attractive features as she scrutinized him.

'I'm sorry.' Her voice certainly sounded different, but it was indeed Joanna. He did not doubt that. 'I don't think I know you, do I?'

He moved round the car, almost tripping over the kerb as he hauled himself up on to the pavement. Only a couple of yards separated them now. 'You know me, all right,' he leered, wondering why she was carrying those white overalls neatly folded over her arm. Visiting some client, perhaps, whose perverse delight was playing kinky games, and tonight she was going to dress up as a nurse for him. 'You remember me, don't you?'

She was looking at him with narrowed eyes, her brow furrowed. 'Yes, perhaps I do,' she said. 'Aren't you . . . Mr Mannion?'

His own name hit him with force, a shock that sent his brain reeling. He had never told that whore his name, and even if he had he would have used a pseudonym. Christ! It was frightening, here in his own locality.

'That's right.' He moved a step closer. 'Though how you know that is beyond me.'

'I do have a good memory.' Her tone was haughty now. 'And I like to remember all my — '

'Clients?'

'If you like. I call them "patients".'

So it *was* a kinky game, and tonight her role was that of a nurse. But Mike had no time for that sort of play. He was aware of his arousal, the way it dominated him to the exclusion of everything else. 'Come on,' he said in a whisper, 'hop in and we'll take a ride somewhere.'

'How dare you!'

'Come off it!' He was close to her now and his fingers flexed. 'You took *me* for a ride last time. Now it's my turn. Literally. Jump in.'

She turned and was about to run, but he moved faster than he thought he was capable of, grabbing her arm. She struggled; he tightened his grip. 'I paid you a lot of money the last time. Now you're going to earn it, *Joanna*!'

'Let go of me. My name isn't Joanna. I'm going to call the police!'

Instinctively his hand closed over her mouth just as she started to scream. He pulled her to him and felt her body squash against his protruding swollen navel – a moment of agony followed by a deluge of something warm and sticky between their pressed bodies. His lips pursued hers, crushing them as she screamed into his mouth, his fingers tearing at her clothing. Pushing her back through the gateway, he sent them both sprawling on to the gravel but he scarcely noticed the sharp stones. A crazed stag at the rutting stand, he saw Joanna struggling beneath him and that fog closing in as though to hide the obscenity. Damn this bitch of a whore, she was going to earn that thirty quid he had given her the other night!

Doctor Williamson was tired. Any other time he would have taken a nap in the living room, content in the knowledge that he would waken instantly if the telephone rang. But this evening he was troubled, the peace of mind which he habitually enjoyed destroyed by the knowledge of what old Josh Owen had told him. Anybody else, any other time, the doctor would have dismissed it as the wanderings of a dying man in the final stages of senile dementia. But not Josh; the farmer had been alert, was not given to romancing, and the story had a ring of truth to it, even though it was a legend handed down through several generations.

Improbable, nay impossible – unless you had looked upon the festered body of Jim Fitzpatrick! He had seen the way those terrible ulcers pulsed and ate the dead flesh like carnivorous bloated leeches. That made him believe, and he wondered how it was all going to end.

Williamson picked up the phone and dialled. He heard it ringing at the other end, and counted. A dozen rings, and he could safely assume that there would be no reply. But this time he hung on, and on the fifteenth distant *burr-burr* a man's voice answered, slightly irritated at being disturbed from whatever he had been doing. 'Professor Shaw speaking.'

'Don, this is Gerald Williamson.'

'Why, Gerald! Long time, no see. How are you?'

Small talk, chat between old university colleagues, a roundabout way of leading up to the purpose of an unexpected call.

'Don, I want to ask a big favour, strictly off the record,' the doctor was almost humble, for the man he spoke to was an eminent professor who had studied contagious fatal diseases ever since his Cambridge days. Aloof, short-tempered, even as an undergraduate, Shaw never tolerated time-wasters. And this business sounded ridiculous, fanciful, like a far-fetched plot from a science fiction pulp of the thirties, when hack authors could get away with it because medical science was still in its infancy. 'Do you know of any disease, plague, which could devour a corpse and still live on in the gravesoil for several centuries and then become contagious again?' Williamson held his breath, anticipating either ridicule or an angry outburst.

There was only silence; if he had not heard the intake of breath he might have assumed that the professor had replaced the receiver in disgust. It was some seconds before Shaw spoke, and when he did his voice was grave. 'Why?'

'Because I believe it might have happened. Here. I've seen it with my own eyes, and want to trace it. The police are being reticent about it – doubtless tests are being carried out and in due course the truth will emerge. But, for the sake of the people who live in this area, I need to be sure. Now!'

'Gerald, if it was anybody else but you I'd slam the phone down right now. What I'm going to tell you, you won't find in any medical book that has ever been written. In fact, I've never heard it mentioned, and I certainly wouldn't for fear of ridicule. But I *have* read many of the records compiled from the fourteenth century onwards, a lot of them documents handwritten by men whose wisdom was far ahead of their times.

Plagues like the bubonic were commonplace and there were a lot of others brought in by foreign seamen, diseases which are unheard of today. And it is one of those that I read about once, on a scroll of parchment, barely legible, scrawled by an apothecary who himself feared that he had this plague and wished to warn others. He called it *the Festering Death*, and according to him only fire would destroy it. The bodies had to be cremated until, in his words "the sores sizzled and screamed in agony, festers that would live on if they were not burned alive". But I have no evidence to substantiate these writings; I can only tell you what I read. This fellow went on to describe the symptoms, listing them as "festering sores on the body that ate the flesh until death came as a blessed relief, and even then the cancers went on devouring the remaining flesh. The victim underwent hallucinations, agony, became violent in his affliction and suffered from abnormal sexual desires." In those days they put it down to possession by an evil spirit, of course, and in many cases the sufferer was put to death as a result. I cannot for the life of me understand why this terrible plague didn't sweep across Britain. Perhaps it was confined to scattered communities, and the populations were wiped out and forgotten. I don't know. But this chap added as a postscript to his paper that whilst fire destroys the disease completely it will live on in a grave because of the damp earth. It thrives on moisture and needs water to live!'

My God! Williamson gripped the receiver with intensity as he recalled the borehole at Garth Cottage, that deep well, and remembered again Josh Owen's account of how this afflicted traveller was buried 'as deep as a well'. It had to be that, there was no other explanation, logical or illogical. *The Garth well had been the site of the grave of the unknown man who had returned with the Festering Death centuries ago, and the plague had lived on at the bottom of the shaft. And now the Mannions had released it from its incarceration!*

'Thank you.' He sounded exhausted when he spoke again. 'You don't realize how grateful I am to you, my friend. Now, I must hurry. I'll report back to you when I have something which may substantiate the writings of a long-dead apothecary.'

Williamson moved fast in spite of his bulk. He called upstairs to his wife that he had to go out, and any calls were to be relayed to Doctor Bell. Then he hurried to Garth Cottage to warn the Mannions, fearful it might be too late. He remembered the notes Doctor Bell had left about their boils.

He eased the Range Rover down the drive, the laurel branches swishing against its bodywork and slowed habitually on the sharp bend that terminated in the entrance to the main street of Canon Pine. The doctor was ageing, tired, but his reactions were swift as he stood on the brake pedal so that the heavy-duty tyres crunched and slid on loose gravel, and somehow stopped within a foot or so of the couple who lay directly in his path.

A curse escaped his lips, then a premonition brought a pang of fear that flipped his heart. A courting couple, doubtless, who had succumbed to the urge to have intercourse and had chosen his drive because it was screened from the street. He still hoped that it might just be that, until the man eased up off the woman, and he saw that obscene nakedness, the stomach bleeding and oozing sluggish pus from the gaping wound left by the burst, festering ulcer. His face was vaguely familiar through the contortions as he crouched and stood at bay like a cornered beast of the wild.

The doctor's eyes flicked to the woman, who lay on her back, her scratched and gouged flesh visible through the tattered remains of a summer dress, her head lolling at an unnatural angle so that he was unable to see her features. But when he saw the spotless white receptionist's overall lying, still folded, by her side, he knew.

Merciful God, he was too late, after all! Mannion was a victim of the ancient Festering Death – and he had come here in his hour of agony and murdered Susan Willis, the doctor's part-time secretary and receptionist!

17

Holly panicked, blindly. Suddenly all cohesion had left her. She only knew that Mike was missing, that that *thing* had come up out of the well again. It was responsible for his disappearance – had it snatched him, taken him back down to those foul dark depths? Anything was possible. She almost screamed, but it was Nick's presence that choked back the rising screech of hysteria.

'Come on.' He seemed to have difficulty speaking, and lisped badly. 'Let's go and look for him. I'll search outside, you check the house.'

That made sense; with an effort she pulled herself together. She nodded, and made for the stairs. Of course, Mike could be upstairs, in the bathroom, in the bedroom, anywhere. There was no point in having hysterics until it was confirmed that he really was not anywhere to be found.

For a few seconds she was nearly composed again, but halfway up the narrow flight of stairs the pain hit her. It was as though the base of her spine was burning and a fire was consuming her body, scorching into it. Some thick warm fluid was flowing, saturating her pants. She clapped a hand behind her, and felt it squelch on sodden denim. Now that scream left her lips as the agony exploded, eating right into her bowels as if some carnivorous reptile had found an orifice and was intent upon devouring her intestines. She clung on to the stair rail as she almost fell. God, that boil had burst with a vengeance!

She recalled the time many years before when she had once burst a boil, the excruciating pain for a minute or two, the flood of pus. And after that it had been all right; a swab of cotton wool soaked in TCP, and she was fine. She hoped that was what had happened now. I'll be okay, she told herself. I just have to put up with it for a short while.

She made it to the bedroom. Mike wasn't there, but she had known all along that he would not be. For some reason he was no longer a priority; she tugged off her clothes, smelled them, felt the sliminess of the stinking matter on her fingers. Near panic again, she grabbed the hand mirror, holding it so that she could see her rear reflected in the full-length wardrobe glass.

Holy Mother! She stared at what the two mirrors showed her: firm buttocks that were no longer recognizable as her own; they were smeared with blood-streaked pus, and where the sore had been there was now a gaping, ragged hole from which crept a steady surge of glutinous matter, trickling down the backs of her shapely legs. She dropped the small mirror and heard the glass crack as it hit the bare floorboards. Seven years' bad luck; it seemed hers had arrived all at once.

Then she caught sight of her face and recoiled from the haggard, wizened reflection. She thought for one moment that there was another woman in the room, and prayed to God that there was – a crone with sunken cheeks, eyes that burned out of hollowed sockets, and cracked lips with twin streams of mucus running down on to them from flared nostrils. *No, don't let it be. Let it be somebody else!*

Looking about her, she tried to will this awful witch-like apparition to materialize out of the shadowy corners of the bedroom. But in the end she had to accept that there was nobody here except herself. The diseased thing which lived down the well shaft had taken her, infected her, claimed her for one of its tortured, demented victims!

She staggered through to the bathroom and began to

splash her naked body with cold water in an attempt to cool it, shuddering as she remembered where that water came from. It was contaminated, whether or not the health inspector passed it as pure. Diseased.

She went downstairs, clambering down like the hag she had become. The steps were slippery with the poison seeping from her. Standing in the kitchen, leaning against the scrubbed pine table, wheezing for breath, tasting the foul saliva in her mouth, she mouthed her pleas for help.

She heard Nick coming across the patio, his feet scuffing, scraping. Then he coughed, retching, before entering the room. She *knew* without looking up, knew that it had got him, too.

It did not come as a shock; she had expected it. The evil force had left its subterranean well and taken them all with alarming, unbelievable rapidity. None of them could hope to escape. Wherever Mike was, it had got him, too.

Nick looked at her, but took time focusing his gaze. His feverish eyes narrowed in an expression of revulsion, but it was gone as quickly as it came.

'It took us all,' Holly croaked.

'Yes.' He lurched forward and stood at the opposite end of the table, holding on to it. 'I haven't felt well for days, you know.' His eyes travelled up and down her naked body, possibly wondering if she was the same woman who had seduced him. Then he smiled. 'Well, we're all the same now, so we'd better make the best of it.'

'I'm going to ring for Doctor Williamson.' She turned towards the phone.

'It won't do any good. He didn't help the others, did he?'

'He only saw Fitzpatrick, and the fellow was already dead. What else can we do?'

He shrugged his shoulders and watched her dialling. She leaned on the wall, holding the receiver as though it weighed several kilos. The phone was ringing at the other end, on and on, purring like a contented cat in her ear. At last she replaced the receiver. 'Nobody's answering. Perhaps the phone is out of order.'

'I didn't find your husband,' he said, 'but the car's gone.'

'So he fled the battlefield.' There was contempt in her voice. 'He deserted the dying in their hour of need.'

'He might have gone to get help.'

'He might have.' She did not sound convinced. The floor was slippery beneath her feet where her poisoned juices still trickled. 'Nick, you know what we discussed, about the cement?'

'Yes.' He was lisping more than ever now, but she dared not mention his speech impediment, remembering how Jim Fitzpatrick had been that time.

'I think we should go ahead with the idea.'

'No point. It's too late.'

'We might save other lives. Bury the bastard, whatever it is, and concrete it in.'

'We'd still have to wait for tomorrow. The quarry will be closed now.'

'Couldn't you *mix* up some cement?'

'Christ, it'll take tons of the stuff. We'll need a ready-mix; it would be impossible without it.'

Silence. 'We've got to destroy it!' There was a pathetic determination about her now. Exhausted, she sank down into the nearest chair. 'That borehole is its lair, it *lives* down there. All we need to do is to block it up, seal it in forever. It's *our* fault, Mike's and mine – we let it out by drilling an open shaft. But we could trap it back in there, if we had the means.'

Nick Paton was thoughtful. He rubbed his mouth with the back of his hand, then protruded his tongue and plucked at it with his fingers as if he had an irritating hair lodged on it. Holly recoiled, wanting to avert her eyes, but it was as if that swollen tongue with its ugly protuberances hypnotized her.

'Nick!' She found her voice, a kind of terrified squeak.

'Sure, I've got 'em.' He gave a laugh that sounded as

though he was vomiting. 'You're right, we've got to finish the thing off once and for all. I've an idea. . . .' He lapsed back into silence, head buried in his hands. She did not know whether he was deep in thought or pain. After some minutes he looked up, and there was an expression in his eyes which took some moments to identify. Hatred! 'I'll fix the fucker!'

'Good.' She waited for him to go on.

'Suppose we *poisoned* it, like it's poisoned us!'

'How?'

'I know a gamekeeper, about a mile from here. He uses Cymag, cyanide gas, to kill rabbits when they breed too quickly. I've read that they also use it for poaching salmon – tip it in the river and wait at the other end until all the dead fish come floating down.'

'But we might poison the underground stream and kill half the villagers of Garth!'

'Apparently not.' He did his best to smile. 'It evaporates or dissolves – I'm not sure which – after a time and becomes harmless. It's worth a try, anyway.'

'If you're sure.' She sounded doubtful.

'I'll go and scrounge a can off him.' With difficulty he rose to his feet.

'I'd better come with you. Will either of us be able to drive?'

'You stop here, I can manage.' He made it to the door. Outside, the evening shadows were lengthening and the sun was already out of sight behind the mountains. 'I won't be long.'

She sat there and listened to him starting up the van. The engine was roaring because he was having difficulty with the accelerator pedal. Jerking, stalling; starting again. She held her breath as she heard him pull out into the lane, and tensed as she remembered what had happened to Bill Cole. Then she was following Nick's progress with her ears until finally she could hear him no more. *Pray God he comes back with the cyanide and it does the trick.*

*

It was too good to be true. The van was back – she heard it clip that leaning gatepost with a metallic clang, then slowing. One last roar of the indignant engine before it died. A door slammed. Slow, dragging footsteps were coming towards the cottage, scraping on the patio.

Holly closed her eyes. It could not be Nick, she had not expected to see him again. But it was, labouring under the weight of a can that resembled a catering tin of instant coffee in appearance. He set it on the table and sat down.

'Got it!' There was triumph in his tone. 'There was nobody around at the keeper's cottage so I just went into the shed and helped myself. Sam'll probably never miss it. Now we'd better get it open. Damn, I'll have to go back to the van and fetch a screwdriver!'

'Use this.' She opened the cutlery drawer of the table and handed him a serving spoon.

The sweat stood out on his brow, glistening in the fading daylight as he exerted all his waning strength with the improvised lever under the lip of the can. A twang sounded as the metal capitulated. 'There! Better not open it right up in case we get a whiff of the fumes.'

'Nick. . . .' Holly's voice shook, her splayed fingers covered her disfigured features. 'Nick, we're both going to die . . . aren't we?'

'Yes.' He knew there was no point in lying at this late stage. 'There's nothing we can do about it but, like you, I'd feel happier if we fixed that well before we go.'

'Don't you think we could drive somewhere for help? *After* we've done the job.'

'Maybe.' He didn't think so. He had struggled to the gamekeeper's cottage and back, mounting the verge on both sides of the road innumerable times. It was sheer luck that he had not met another vehicle. There was nobody in at the doctor's surgery, or the phone would have been answered, and he was in no state to drive further afield. His eyesight was dimming by the hour;

before morning, if he still lived, he was sure that he would be totally blind.

She was looking at him in the half-light, the falling dusk hiding her expression from him. Pity had turned to anger, to resentment. He didn't want to go for help, he was stalling, she realized. He was enjoying the thought of death because his brain was twisted. It was after *he* had done something at the well that its occupant had come and taken them for its own! *His* fault! She only had Nick's word for it that Mike had gone off in the car. . . . The bastard! It was all beginning to fit – he was a crazed psychopath who had hit upon a way to kill them all, then take his own life! Maybe some kind of bacteria had been introduced into the well *after* it had been drilled. By *him*! Holly trembled. Reasoning wasn't easy, but she had it now. What have you done with my husband? she wondered. Where's his body? *I know, you've dropped him down the borehole!*

'Let's go and fix this thing, then.' She spoke calmly, almost normally. 'The sooner, the better. Before it kills again.'

She watched as he struggled with the can of poison and almost dropped it. Yes, she was sure he had treated the well in the first place. The remedy was supplied just *too* easily.

Outside it was almost dark, a balmy summer's evening. She was sweating profusely. That cancer on her spine was still seeping, leaving thick droplets on the ground in her wake as she shambled after Nick through a land of silhouettes. The trees and bushes were still bent under the weight of dried slurry; only a thunderstorm would wash them clean. She found herself listening, hoping. No sound, not even the twittering of birdlife, only a roaring in her ears. The countryside had been deserted by Nature's creatures because even they recognized a place of death and fled from it. But it didn't matter now, she thought. Nothing mattered except. . . .

'Here we are!' There was relief in his voice as he

reached the ragged crater top, clanked his burden down and knelt beside it, exhausted. He sniffed the air. 'Seems pure enough now. Maybe we're too late and it really has gone.'

'We thought that before,' she whispered. 'But it came back again. It's down there, all right, I know. Hurry, let's finish the job. What are you waiting for?' He was procrastinating because he did not want to destroy his maniacal handiwork, she thought. He wanted whatever he had dropped down there to kill, and kill again.

He struggled with the lid. Even though it was already loosened he barely had the strength now to prize it off, clawing at it with his fingernails. Suddenly the top gave, shot from Nick's grasp, spun away and rolled, clinking, rattling and going over the edge. They heard it spinning its way down into the depths, pinging from side to side as it went. Until finally there was the faintest of splashes.

'You bloody fool!' she hissed. 'Now you've warned it!'

'Don't be bleedin' stupid! What d'you think it is, some kind of bogeyman, or maybe a wild animal?'

'Perhaps.' Her fists clenched. She was kneeling behind him. 'Who knows? Go on, tip that stuff in!'

He crawled closer to the brink, then hung back, remembering the last time when that cold foul stench that was an embodiment of living evil had come up at him, *touched* him. His fingers trembled as he edged the canister closed and started to tip it.

Something showered from the container, stark white in the deepening darkness, fine powder that rustled as it spilled out. Hissing over the edge, it reminded him of the near-silent swish of gently falling snowflakes – so soft, so deadly.

They were both listening. It was like sand avalanching in the dunes, spilling a steady stream until at last the tin was empty. He resisted the temptation to throw it after its contents; like his torch, it might incur the wrath of whatever lurked below.

In their imagination they heard it fizzing in the water

like Epsom salts in a tumbler, bubbling and foaming, dissolving, giving off its deadly gas.

'We'd better move away,' he said in hushed tones.

That was when the idea came to her, a spontaneous decision that required no deliberation. The plumber had instigated this foul scheme; maybe Bhopal or some other major disaster had given him the idea, a way to kill. Now it was *his* turn!

Holly exerted her remaining strength, pushed hard with the flat of both hands and caught her companion off balance. He tottered, flailed his arms, grabbed for her and missed. His scream reminded her of the terrified squeals of a rabbit in the final throes of myxomatosis.

She caught a final glimpse of him, a shape that was darker than the surrounding shadows, as he slid over the edge.

Then he was gone.

Nick fell feet first, slipping down the stygian shaft as though he had stepped into a lift on the fifteenth floor only to find it wasn't there. Going down, down. And down.

He gathered speed, then checked as his body struck protruding rocks, dislodging soil, screaming again because he knew, even in his tortured brain, that bones were breaking, snapping and shattering. The never-ending fall might go right down to the bowels of hell itself.

For him, time had ceased to exist. He might already be dead and this was what it was like: hell, where you fell for eternity, everlasting vertigo, struggling to breathe although it did not matter whether you did or not, eternally waiting for a shuddering impact that would never come.

Cold air rushed past him, freezing fingers stroked his plummeting body as it hurtled on downwards. And when, finally, he hit the bottom it was almost an anticlimax. There was a splash, and water closed over him, slowing his fall; his broken legs hit something soft and he was catapulted back up. Half-submerged, he floated in a metre of icy water, barely alive – but still death eluded him cruelly.

He opened his eyes, and was surprised to find that he could see, that it was no longer impenetrable darkness all around him. The rough walls glistened with a strange and frightening glow, a gentle light that enabled him to make out his surroundings. Just as he had imagined, feared, he was in the water at the bottom of a well. *But there was something else. . . .*

It rested on a shelf about a metre away from him, level with his head and shoulders. He could see it plainly, for it was this object which gave off the eerie luminous glow which glinted on the sides of the rocky shaft and showed him the blue well liner with the submersible pump attached to it. Shapeless, indefinable, it was just a glutinous morass about the size of an adult tortoise that breathed and pulsed. Wheezing softly, it reminded him of a gigantic blob of old man's phlegm spat upon a pavement. The cold heart pumped even though it did not have a body, the being lived and thrived in the cold dampness of a deep well.

And gave off a nauseating smell of putrefaction.

18

Doctor Williamson sat dazed behind the wheel of his Range Rover. He tried not to believe what his eyes saw, and told himself it was some kind of a nightmare that would melt into a bad memory when he woke up. Or else it was caused by the heat – an hallucination, a kind of mirage. But deep down he knew that it was reality.

The girl lying on the gravel, her head twisted at an unnatural angle, was undoubtedly Susan Willis – blonde and beautiful, and only nineteen. The grief welled up inside him and he almost sobbed. Instead he fought for professionalism, the one factor that kept doctors sane. In circumstances such as this, he remembered, you strived to become a kind of medical machine and adopted a procedure. He had once written it down on paper back in his college days. First, a body was only pronounced dead when you ascertained that it had no heartbeat, no pulse. You attempted to restart the heart, and only when that failed did you accept the finality. He eased the driver's door open. There was still hope.

He found himself staring at Mike Mannion, telling himself that it could not possibly be the man from Garth Cottage. His gaze rested on the weeping stomach wound, the gaping hole where the navel ulcer had burst and spewed its stinking poison down to the groin. Williamson heaved once, then got himself under control again. Doctor Bell had examined that sore only a short time ago, and he had tried to convince himself and his patient that it was no more than a boil that might go septic; he had stalled and hoped, because he wasn't sure. Every medic gave himself time. Now time had run out on his patient.

Mannion's lips were ulcerated, too, moving as though he was attempting to speak, but all he could manage were wheezes. Dribbling pus hung in strings and swung to and fro. His eyes had glazed over and seemed to have shrunk back into their sockets. In all probability the man's vision was severely restricted, Williamson suspected, and he might even be blind. Pathetic, no longer a physical threat, he was standing there because his brain had wound down.

Williamson turned his attention to the girl at his feet. Dead, of course, she could not be otherwise, with a broken neck and those strangulation marks on her throat.

He knelt down and felt for a pulse, knowing there

would be none. In despair, he put his lips to hers, realizing that it was futile, but he had to satisfy his own conscience. *I hope you're watching, Mannion, because this is your doing!* No, it wasn't Mannion's fault. The professor's words echoed in Gerald Williamson's brain: *the Festering Death!* The doctor straightened up and turned back to the man who still stood there, not crouching at bay now, slumped but still on his feet, totally unaware, mentally and physically drained, an empty shell. A zombie, in fact.

'Mannion?' Of course, there would be no reply. The man's brain was gone. Williamson could see those pulsating sores now; they were growing by the second, burrowing up out of the flesh like an infestation of leeches, sucking blood and devouring human meat. 'Can you hear me, Mannion?'

Not so much as a grunt, just a vacant expression on the disfigured features. Williamson looked about him; there was nobody in sight. He heard footsteps on the pavement beyond the laurels and rhododendrons, hurrying past the drive entrance, not stopping. He was alone with this demented, diseased creature in human shape. That in itself was awful enough, but Mannion was beyond help and would surely be dead within the hour. With a start, the doctor realized that his duty was to the living, those who still might be saved – like Holly Mannion, doubtless blissfully unaware of her husband's fate, alone in the cottage with that terrible, inexplicable force that still lived deep down in the old well shaft. He had to move fast.

Williamson straightened up, stretched out an arm, closed his eyes momentarily as his fingers made contact with Mannion's arm, felt the heat of fevered flesh and grasped it gently but firmly. Mannion swayed, almost toppling.

'Mannion.' The doctor felt the need to talk even though he was probably neither heard nor understood. 'I want you to come with me, old chap. You're ill –

probably the heat. I'm going to take you indoors and find you somewhere to lie down. You can rest there. Then I'll be away for a while, and when I get back you'll probably feel better. If not, then I'll give you something to make you better.' *Liar*, he accused himself.

He began to lead the sick man, a tottering step at a time, pulling him along, hoping that he wouldn't fall, because he would never have been able to get him back on to his feet. He could not leave him where he was in case somebody came in through the gate. He would need to move Susan's body, too; drag it into the bushes like a murderer trying to conceal the corpse of his victim, simply because he could not move the Range Rover until he did so. Then he would ring the police and let them sort things out whilst he rushed to Garth Cottage. Any questions that needed to be answered could be answered afterwards. Life came before the Festering Death.

The doctor glanced up at the windows of the house, fearing his wife might be looking out; he breathed an audible sigh of relief when he saw no face at the latticed panes. *Spare her this, I pray you, God!*

Into the reception area, now sliding Mannion along the polished linoleum floor as one might move a heavy filing cabinet to a new position. The first door was the waiting room, the second had a brass plaque which read 'Treatment Room' – a kind of minor operating theatre where the GP removed warts and stitched cuts which were not serious enough for the hospital in town. There was a lock, a means of preventing anybody from wandering in there by mistake. He opened the Treatment Room door.

With four whitewashed walls, a washbasin, a medicinal cupboard and a moveable padded treatment couch in the centre, it was basic but sufficient. Ideal, right now.

'Now, let's have you lying up on this.' Williamson was sweating heavily and he felt suddenly weak. 'Up we go old chap!'

One last supreme effort, and he pushed the limp figure on to the couch, then heaved it from the legs. The trolley moved, its well-oiled wheels taking it against the near wall, where it wedged. Williamson grunted as he swung the patient on to the upholstery and managed to catch him before he fell off the other side. 'Bravo!' He bent double, feeling sick, but it passed.

Mannion lay on his back and might have been staring up at the ceiling if his eyes had not been dead. The torso was heaving, the mucus bubbled in the nostrils. That stench was growing stronger now, Williamson noticed, its foulness emanating from the open abdominal wound as yellow and pink pus began to roll on to the pseudo-leather covering. The doctor turned his head away, hoping that it would all be over by the time he returned. Just a death certificate to write out. Cause of death . . . *the Festering*!

He stepped out into the hall, locked the door behind him, and as an afterthought pocketed the key. He could not take any chances. He felt his chest pounding and hoped that it was nothing serious. He wasn't used to such exertions. He went outside and walked towards the parked vehicle. The girl was lying where he had left her, only her face was turned towards him – probably because he had moved her to examine her, he remembered. Her wide open blue eyes seemed to plead with him, and the parted lips looked as if they were struggling to speak. Which he knew was nonsense because she was dead.

He moved her gently back into the bushes and covered her with the spotless white overall that had fallen by her side – a shroud. It seemed a futile thing to do but he felt he owed it to her, a touch of dignity. The police would not approve; he should have known better and left her where she had fallen.

He made one last trip back to the house and used the telephone in reception. A quick call – there was no time to waste – but he had to inform the law at this stage, as the consequences might be serious if he did not.

He almost ran back to the Range Rover. He had

wasted too much time already, and Holly Mannion's life was at stake.

Holly had gone back indoors. There was nothing to stop out here for, she thought. Nick was dead, and they would never find him down there. Not that she cared if they did because it would be too late for all of them by then.

She had difficulty in walking and had to clutch at everything she bumped into to remain upright. *Christ*, she felt ill. Not so much the pain now, more a kind of numbness, like when she sat on the loo too long and her thighs lost their feeling. Instinctively she felt behind her, running her fingers through the spongy, slimy morass where her spine ended. There was a deep hole but she had not the courage to penetrate it with her hand, fearing it might go right into her bowels. It smelled as if it did.

She made for the stairs, not bothering to switch on the light. Her vision was impaired. She had been aware of that for some time and knew she was going blind. Darkness was a relief in a way.

She made her way slowly upstairs, crawling on all fours when she neared the top in case she fell back, slithering on to the polished bare boards of the landing. She went through to the bedroom; she needed to rest, to sleep. Perhaps when she awoke, she thought, everything would be all right and it had only been a bad dream.

She pulled herself upright and waited for her balance to return. Something shone silvery in the darkness, a vertical oblong that glinted evilly, watching her. The wardrobe mirror! It had a kind of hypnotic effect on her, commanded her attention, penetrated her confused thoughts.

She stared, but all she saw was an outline, a reflection of shadows, and could barely make out her own silhouette among them. That way she looked normal; it hid everything that she did not want to see. I don't want to see any more, she thought. *You have to. Put the light on!*

No! But she knew she would, just like the victim of

some terrible accident compelled to view their own injuries, fearing the worst but hoping for the best. She wouldn't rest until she'd *seen*.

Reaching up for the light pull by the bed, hesitating with her fingers touching the cord, she hoped that perhaps it would not work because the bulb had blown or maybe there had been a power cut. She knew there was only one way to find out.

Blinding white light dazzled her even through her fogged vision. She clasped her hands over her eyes trying to shut it out, recoiling. She grabbed at the pull again, but it was swinging, avoiding her clutching fingers, to and fro, back and forth. Her arm was tiring and she was forced to lower it. She rested her back against the wall, and eventually opened her eyes.

The mirror shining at her had taken on the shape of a living, moving human being – a naked girl with firm breasts and wide hips, her body unblemished, trembling with fear and then with elation. Seeing what she wanted to see, scarcely recognizing herself, Holly remembered how she had looked the last time, and continued searching for those disfigurations – but did not find them. They were gone! Turning her back, twisting her head, she strained to view the place where it had all started, but there was nothing there. She was laughing and crying.

She sat down on the edge of the bed. She felt no pain, just a numbness; but she knew that was a small price to pay. Hysterical now, she lay back – and when she reached up again she found the light pull and plunged the room back into darkness.

Her mind flicked from one memory to another: Eaton, Fitzpatrick, Bennion . . . Nick Paton! Oh, God, how she hated him for what he had done, and herself for seducing him. And Mike, too – she was well rid of him. She hoped he was dead, wherever he was, because that way she had a clean slate, a fresh start. Tomorrow everything would be all right.

It was some time before she realized that there was no

longer the silence of a balmy summer's evening outside. A kind of swishing sound had started, like the wind getting up, soughing through the slurry-coated foliage. Or the rushing of water, she thought – perhaps the waste pipe in the adjacent field pumping again in an effort to rid the well of the filth that was alive in it. Continuous, escalating, rushing, the noise was growing in volume, frightening.

And then that familiar odour of putrefaction and evil came seeping in through the gaps in the badly fitted window.

19

Dusk came swiftly then turned to darkness with an alarming rapidity. It was always the same, summer or winter, in those small villages situated beneath the towering Bryn mountains. Once the sun had dipped behind the topmost peaks, the day surrendered to night.

Doctor Williamson was suddenly aware that it was dark. He had switched on the sidelights of the Range Rover as he pulled out of Canon Pine, but a mile further down the road he put on the headlights, their powerful twin beams reflecting the drought-ravaged countryside almost like an unexpected fall of snow. Eerie; he shuddered. It was like one of those dreams where he was trying to go somewhere but got nowhere, ending up exactly where he had begun. The drama at the surgery seemed to have lasted for hours; he had no idea how long it had taken.

The road was familiar, but now he saw it differently. This was no routine call, not even one of those emergencies which he got from time to time when somebody in one of the outlying homesteads had a heart attack or an appendicitis. It was frightening; in a way he did not want to arrive at his destination and almost wished that he had waited for the police and accompanied them. But it was his duty to save lives, and every second he delayed could mean the difference between life and death.

Garth village. He found himself slowing subconsciously as he saw the 30 mph sign, then accelerated again. This was no time to be obeying the law to the letter. On through the village. There was nobody about. Lights were showing in the windows of houses and cottages, cars were parked in drives and in the main street. It was if the entire population was skulking indoors because they knew of the evil which had manifested itself.

The Mannions' drive. He was turning in when his lights picked up the van blocking the way, forcing him to break sharply. That was the plumber's vehicle – he knew it only too well. Momentarily relieved because he wasn't alone and neither was Holly, he wondered if perhaps everything would be all right, after all.

He switched off the engine but left the headlights on, and sat for a moment, scrutinizing the scene below him. In the overgrown garden was a small hollow resembling a building site with its mounds of rubble and equipment. It was like a deep dark pool, which in fact it was. His mouth went dry at the thought of the long drop down through the earth to the foul water at the bottom, the very place where this ancient evil had spawned. Professor Shaw had not ridiculed the idea, and there could not possibly be any other explanation.

Doctor Williamson got out, leaving the door open and the lights burning to show him the way. He moved stiffly, slowly. There were no lights showing in the cottage; perhaps there was nobody at home – which would solve a lot of problems. But he knew it was not so. A kind of foreboding told him the evil was still here. *He could smell it!*

The stench of rotting corpses reminded him of an exhumed graveyard, the atmosphere heavy with disease. He remembered that awful day during his war years as an army MD when he had moved among the dead and wounded on the battlefield, the cries of anguish mingling with that unmistakable smell of death.

At first he thought it was his memory playing tricks on him, that low moan which filled the air, the wail that grew louder by the second – the agonized cry of a tortured soul, the ultimate in pain and despair. It vibrated the atmosphere, penetrated his brain and made him clutch his ears in an attempt to shut it out. He resisted the urge to flee back to his vehicle, to run from this place and leave the occupants to their fate. The sound resembled a rising wind and yet there was none, not so much as a gentle breeze. Coming at him, invisible demons attempted to drive him back. *Begone!* Fighting against this inexplicable force, he was groping his way towards that dreadful hole in the ground. Knowing that the heart of this terrible malevolence pumped at the bottom of that dark cold shaft.

A metre from the brink he halted, feeling the icy coldness, the penetrating damp of an opened grave. Labouring to breathe, he crawled now in case he fell. *And then he heard the voice, the whisper that magnified and echoed down in those depths.*

'*Help me!*'

The wail, human and yet inhuman, was vaguely familiar. It was certainly not Holly Mannion. Who, then? Nick Paton, the plumber!

'Paton . . . can you hear me?' The doctor's cry was little more than a whisper, whipped away by the force which tore at him. Knowing the plumber would not hear him, he tried again. 'Paton, is that you?'

This time there was no reply, just a distant groaning. It had to be the plumber because his van was here. He had slipped and fallen down . . . *there*! Oh, merciful Lord, Paton was surely close to death. It would need ropes and potholing experts to bring the injured man to the surface. Williamson wondered how long the police would be. In the meantime where was Mrs Mannion? Was she down there, too?

'Good evening, Doctor Williamson!'

He started, turned and saw that the porch light was on, illuminating the patio. Framed in the doorway was a figure that was no more than a silhouette against the glare of the overhead bulb, unrecognizable at this distance – but he knew it was Holly. He knew also that she was stark naked.

His initial embarrassment was swamped by a flood of fear. There was something decidedly odd about her: her posture, the way her neck craned forward as though she was . . . not just watching him but *lusting* for him, waiting because she knew that he would come to her.

He scrambled up, aware of his ungainliness, his clumsiness. He was breathing heavily and he could feel the way his temples pounded; there was a noise in his ears like rushing water, as if that strange sound which he had heard a few minutes ago was now concentrated inside his head. Instinctively he dusted himself down, then walked unsteadily towards Garth Cottage.

'I'm glad you've come, Doctor.' Her voice sounded *almost* normal. But not quite. 'I had hoped that perhaps my husband had called to see you, but obviously he hasn't, otherwise you would not be here now. You see, Mike is rather poorly – an ulcer on his stomach.'

Williamson stopped, then recoiled. Oh, God above, he could see Holly clearly now, *a wretched crone who had aged decades these last few hours, her nakedness a mass of bulbous sores that spread and weeped, the pus seeming to carry the virus like molten lava, burning the flesh as it trickled thickly. Festering lips were drawn back in a wolfish snarl, and nostrils bubbled with liquid mucus. Eyes burned deep in their blackened sockets, and those wretched hands smoothed their way down her wasted stomach, meeting in the warmth of her pressed thighs. A caricature of femininity, there was no mistaking her provocativeness; she was a filthy slag offering her body for a pittance on a street corner.*

'Mrs Mannion — '

'Holly, please . . . Gerald!'

He stiffened, stepped back and glanced up the drive. A pair of dazzling eyes blinded him temporarily; the Range Rover was like a hunting beast of the night which had spotted its prey and sought to hypnotize it, a stoat mesmerizing a hapless coney whilst it closed in for the kill, holding him there. He heard Holly's stealthy padded footsteps and caught a whiff of her presence as though she had arisen from her foul bed in her stinking lair. He felt the clammy grip of her outstretched hand on his own.

'Come inside, Gerald,' she whispered, and began pulling him towards the door.

'You're ill.' He was standing inside the kitchen now. 'Very ill. I think we ought to call an ambulance.'

'Oh, no.' The stretching of those diseased lips was meant to be a reassuring smile. 'I have been ill but I'm all right now. You see, it's all Mike's fault.'

'Mike is. . . .'

'Dead?'

'Seriously ill. Like yourself. He . . . killed a young girl!'

He had meant to shock her, using the only weapon he could muster, but it failed miserably. The sweat-soaked skin on her brow tried to furrow as she smiled again. 'I'm not surprised. You see, his passion for city whores brought this upon us all. It will destroy us. I'm glad that he's suffering, too.'

'What . . . whatever to you mean?'

'Let me tell you.' She led him across to a chair and pushed him down on to it. 'Mike went away. To London. When he returned and I saw that ulcer on his belly, I knew full well where he had got it. *From lying with dirty whores!* He came back, pretending that everything was all right, and in the meantime infected me. And others. The plague is spreading fast. The plumber caught it. I did the only possible thing in the circumstances: I buried him deep – very deep. But the grave . . . the well shaft, must be filled in before it is too late. I would have buried Mike, too, but he must have guessed and fled. Wherever he is, I beg of you to bring him back here so that we can inter him. But perhaps we are too late and the disease is already raging through the community.'

Williamson's sweat had chilled and he shivered uncontrollably. He was hearing yet another version of the legend which old Josh Owen had related to him, the one passed down from father to son over several generations. A modern-day version of the return of the prodigal son, the plague that could not die except by fire. *The Festering Death was risen from its burial place!*

She was leaning back against the table in a lewd stance with legs wide apart, her blistered fingers pulling at soft flesh. Grinning horribly, she was willing him to watch and be seduced.

'I. . . I'd better go and get Mike.' He made as if to rise, but she pushed him back into his seat, and laughed. The ruse had not fooled her.

'No, doctor. I think it is too late, anyway, from what you tell me. Let us go out there and fill the grave in.'

'Paton isn't dead. I heard him groaning at the bottom of the shaft.'

'You heard *something*, doctor. But not Nick! The thing that lives down there is hungering to feed again. We must give it flesh, human flesh, or else it will rise and go in search of living bodies!'

He swallowed. She's crazy, he thought. The plague has taken her mind. Listening above the roaring in his ears, he was hoping to hear the sound of approaching vehicles. But there was nothing. How much longer were the police going to be?

'Come on.' She was grasping his wrist, struggling to get him up on to his feet. 'We have work to do and there isn't much time left.'

'How are we going to fill in the well?'

'With shovels. There are a couple lying out there.'

'Impossible. It would take days, even weeks.'

'We shall manage it.' She coughed, and something landed stickily on the floor. She was dragging him now, with an urgency about her that bordered on panic.

Her strength was waning. Like her husband, she was running out of time. So far she had had an advantage over him, with her pathetic state and her mania. But Williamson knew that he had to act fast, for part of what she said was true – *there was a living disease at the bottom of that borehole that had to be destroyed.*

Even as they stepped outside he turned on her, twisted the arm which she held him behind her back, grabbed the other and jerked it upwards. Holly screamed, a yell of pain and frustration, and anger because he had dared to turn on her. Her head came round and her teeth snapped, then ground together. She hissed, dribbling revolting pus on to her ravaged bosom. She struggled, but she was too weak even for an ageing man, cursing as he pushed her before him. Making inarticulate protests, she slumped back against him as soon as they were indoors again, but he was not deceived. The sudden strength of the demented was not to be underestimated.

He looked around and saw a cupboard beneath the stairs, its door hanging open. That would do – it would have to, he decided. He shoved her towards it, thrust her into its opening and she sprawled across an array of buckets and cleaning materials. He slammed the flimsy door and pushed the wooden catch into place. As he leaned back against it, he allowed himself just one sigh of relief – and then he was moving towards the outer door.

An idea which had only just come to him renewed his ebbing strength. Shuffling, shambling, he hurried towards the Range Rover, those twin eyes blinding him as if it, too, was on *their* side. Scrabbling in the back, he found what he was looking for – a red canister with a closed spout. Its contents sloshed about inside as he hurried on down to the hollow below.

He knelt and fumbled with the spring catch that held the collapsible spout closed, snagging a fingernail even as he managed to prise it free. Lying full length, he held the nozzle over the brink, tipping the jerry can and hearing liquid gurgle out of it. The stench drowned the sharp odour of the petrol – that putrefying smell was beginning again. *The Festering was stirring from its temporary slumber, coming up the shaft towards him as if it knew!*

The can was empty. He let it fall and listened as it went clanking downwards. He could hear that groaning again, a wheezing that sounded as if the wind was rising, or an ancient entity was crying its anguish aloud, screeching its hatred. *Hungering for living flesh.*

The doctor's fingers trembled and the matchbox rattled as he drew it from his trouser pocket. He sent a briar pipe rolling across the hard ground, and matches spilled from the open box, but somehow he held one, rasped it on the emery paper, and a miniature flare fell burning into the mouth of the well. Another. And another. He was striking them as fast as he could find them, until at last the box in his hand was empty. He waited, face pressed against the ground. Just one match, he thought. That was all that was needed, a tiny flame to ignite the fumes down below. But perpaps they had been extinguished on their fall, and it was all in vain.

The stench was growing stronger. He felt it in his throat, in his nostrils, a living force that tried to suffocate him, making him cough and retch. And all the time that cry from down below was getting louder.

Then suddenly the ground and sky seemed to explode. Williamson saw the gush of flame even through closed eyes, a tongue of fire that shot out of the gaping hole like a burning geyser, a subterranean dragon venting its anger on the world above. The dark sky turned orange in a premature fiery dawn.

Then the doctor was clutching his ears again as he heard the screams from below, deafening cries of agony, the shrieking of a burning soul in hell, reaching shrieking pitch, then dying away as the inferno down below took hold. Hell itself was being consumed in its own flames, he thought, as the intense heat surged upwards, and stones cracked and splintered in the walls of the shaft. Black smoke came billowing up, obscuring the myriad of stars, amid the underground roaring and hissing as the cauterization began.

Williamson rolled away and crawled, coughing, towards the cottage. Even as he fought to escape the heat and smoke, he permitted himself a smile and recalled Professor Shaw's words taken from the script of an ancient apothecary: *Only fire can destroy the disease completely.*

Through the eddying smoke he saw the lighted dwelling, the back door still open as he had left it. He headed towards it because there was a telephone in there. He would call the emergency services: fire, police, and an ambulance to take Holly Mannion to. . . .

He was unable to hold back his cry of despair as through the stifling gloom he saw, for the second time that night, the silhouette of a naked woman framed in the doorway. Her shrieks of fury reached him even as she saw his crawling figure. The demented girl had found her last maniacal strength and was heading towards him, brandishing a wood-chopper in her festering hands.

20

For Doctor Williamson it was almost too much of an effort to rise to his feet again. Almost, but not quite. His mind was stronger than his body and forced it to respond one last time, just as Holly Mannion must have done in order to escape from that broom cupboard.

He swayed unsteadily and regained his balance with difficulty. His head felt as if it might burst from the pressure inside it, and there was a tightness akin to a restricting steel band clamping his chest. He knew the signs only too well, and just hoped that he could hang on for a little while longer. He wondered whether it really mattered if he couldn't. The plague which had lived in that well for centuries was surely destroyed by fire forever now; nothing could possibly have survived in that raging inferno below ground.

But the plague *had* survived, right here in front of him, in the grotesque form of a diseased woman brandishing a chopper. It had spawned, and it would live on! All his efforts would have been futile unless. . . .

'You fool!' Holly – he found it almost unbelievable that it was her – stopped a few paces from him. 'See what you have done!'

'I thought you wanted it destroyed.' Keep her talking, he told himself. Play for time. The constriction in his chest had eased a little; he felt he might be all right in a few moments.

'*Not now!*' She threw back her head and gave a laugh that rattled the phlegm in her throat. 'Once I did, but that was before I understood. It came up and took me but it did not *destroy* me as it did the others. I recovered, and I am its Chosen One. It has given me immortality in return for keeping the plague alive! I shall live while others die. I can feel its power within me, it has given me a new role, to rule over mankind as a queen.'

You poor fool, he thought. In a matter of hours, perhaps less, you will be dead. He caught his breath as he detected her fetid body odours. The light from the flames were bathing her in an eerie orange glow. Holly Mannion was, in effect, already dead; this creature standing in front of him was surely a she-devil sent by Satan, barely human any longer. Her sores wept, and rivulets of stinking poison ravaged her flesh, leaving a trail of racing cancers in their wake.

'The whores carry it,' she cackled. 'They spread it. That was where Mike got it from. I gave it to Nick . . . *just as I am going to give it to you, doctor!*'

The axe fell from her fingers and thudded to the ground. She did not need it any longer, she decided. It had served its purpose in smashing down the door of her prison. *Now her body was her weapon of death!*

Williamson almost screamed 'keep away', but he knew that she was beyond reasoning now. She dropped into a seductive crouch, a she-hunter stalking her prey, leering. She had to drag her body every inch of the way, her arms reaching out for him.

He eluded her grasp, wondering if he could outrun her, and almost fell. No, he realized his tired old body was as spent as hers, only she was fired with a devilish lust that transcended normal human strength. Now it was a deadly game of chasing and dodging, feinting – and the loser's forfeit was death.

He tried not to envisage her grappling with him, throwing him to the ground and clambering upon him, tearing at his clothing, baring his flesh with those ulcerated fingers. Macabre, terrifying – but in an inexplicable, bizarre way it was also erotic, a primeval urge for mating in its most basic form that went back to the beginning of the world.

He was tiring; his chest was tightening in that invisible vice again. His footwork was clumsy, he was kicking stones and slipping on them. She was toying with him now, displaying her body provocatively. So *sure* of him.

Suddenly they heard a wailing, a sound that seemed to come from nowhere but was everywhere, rising to an incredible ear-bursting pitch, as if a thousand devils were coming out of that fiery well. The noise numbed him, hit him with an almost physical force. And that dancing, flickering orange firelight had become a kaleidoscope of dazzling colours, flashing blue that turned green and then back to orange. Like crazy disco lights that hurt, and he could still see them even when he closed his eyes.

Williamson saw Holly Mannion falter and stagger, her body awash with multi-coloured pus, an optical illusion that transformed her into a shapeless glutinous mass which heaved and pulsed, and steamed opaque putrefaction. Anguished, she was screaming – but it was impossible to hear her cries above this escalation of noise – a cavorting, writhing, demented being who would surely sink down and die at any second.

Realization that it was no army of banshees materializing out of the flames brought relief and euphoria. Instead, a small force of uniformed police officers fought their way through the thick eddying smoke. The authoritative silhouettes came towards the doctor and Holly. And in the far background there was another blare of sirens – ambulance and fire engine, Williamson hazarded a guess.

'Are you all right, doctor?'

Williamson nodded, and out of the corner of his eye he saw Holly miraculously revived. Just as she had seemed about to wilt like a hothouse flower without moisture, she came back to life, one last surge of madness propelling her body beyond the limits of normal human endurance. She straightened up, leaped and ran, a wounded gazelle determined to outdistance an attacking lion. Except that she was heading directly towards that well which now gushed fire like a burning oil geyser instead of water. The lithe figure sprinted, seemingly having thrown off her terrible affliction.

'Stop her!' one of the policeman shouted, and gave pursuit.

'No, let her go,' Doctor Williamson grunted, but nobody heard him. It wouldn't have made any difference to the outcome, anyway. They would not overtake her. Not now.

He was afforded one final glimpse of Holly as the heat drove back her pursuer, and he saw her throw herself forward at the mouth of the borehole in a dive that took her into the very core of those shooting flames. She was outlined for one moment, a plucked fowl roasting on a spit, suspended over the fire and then being sucked down into it. Then gone, forever. It was the only way.

Williamson stood there and watched as the searing heat drove the three policemen still further back. Holly had gone to join Nick Paton down there. The doctor recalled with some relief that Tommy Eaton, Jim Fitzpatrick and Frank Bennion had all been cremated. Now he must ensure that Mike Mannion's corpse was also consumed by fire. Perhaps, as a precaution, he might manage to persuade Susan's parents to have her body disposed of in the same way, too.

Police were moving the obstructing vehicles in order to allow the fire engine access. It did not matter now, the doctor thought, as he allowed a young constable to lead him back to the Range Rover, if they doused the blaze, for the flames had done their work. They had destroyed *the Festering Death*. And cleansed.

It was the only way, as an unknown apothecary had written centuries ago.